About the authors

Polly Clark is the author of *Take Me With You*, a Poetry Book Society Choice and shortlisted for the 2005 TS Eliot Prize, and *Kiss*, a Poetry Book Society Recommendation. She lives on the west coast of Scotland.

Zoe Lambert is a Manchester-based writer. She has an MA in Creative Writing at UEA and she is a PhD student at MMU. Her story, 'Ramshackle' appeared in *Bracket* (Comma). She lectures on the creative writing MA at the University of Bolton and runs the live literature night Verberate.

Jane Rogers is the author of several novels, including *Separate Tracks* (1983); *Her Living Image* (1984), winner of a Somerset Maugham Award; *The Ice is Singing* (1987); *Mr Wroe's Virgins* (1991); *Promised Lands* (1995), winner of the Writers' Guild Award (Best Fiction); *Island* (1999), and *The Voyage Home* (2004). She is the editor of the OUP's *Good Fiction Guide*, and writes for television and radio. Her Channel 4 drama *Dawn and the Candidate* (1989) won a Samuel Beckett Television Award; and her adaptation of *Mr Wroe's Virgins* (1993), directed by Danny Boyle, was nominated for a BAFTA. She teaches on the MA writing course at Sheffield Hallam University. She is a Fellow of the Royal Society of Literature.

ellipsis

#2

Jane Rogers

Polly Clark

Zoe Lambert

First published in Great Britain in 2006 by Comma Press
www.commapress.co.uk

'Road Kill' first appeared in *Hyphen* (Comma, 2003), 'A Quiet Longing' was first podcast as an mp3 as part of Story Bank on www.commapress.co.uk in Dec 2005. 'Grateful' first appeared in *GRANTA 52 (FOOD)*, winter 1995, ed. Ian Jack. 'My Mother and her Sister' first appeared in *The Mail on Sunday Magazine,* ed. Elizabeth Buchan, 1996, and was also broadcast on BBC Radio 4 Morning Story, 10.7.96. 'Salt' first appeared in the novel *Island* (Abacus). 'Conception' first appeared in *Woman's Weekly Fiction Special, No. 47*, 3.10.06.

'These Words are No More Than a Story About a Woman on a Bus' was inspired by an exhibition in the Genocide Victims' Museum in Vilnius, Lithuania, formally the city's KGB prison. The names of the characters are taken from records of partisans who died in the prison, although the story itself is fictional.

ISBN 0-9548280-3-8

Lines from 'Sailing to Byzantium' from THE COLLECTED POEMS OF W.B. YEATS (Wordsworth Poetry Library), published by Wordsworth Editions. Reprinted by permission of AP Watt.

The publisher gratefully acknowledges assistance from the Arts Council England North West, and also the support of Literature Northwest.

Set in Bembo 11/13 by XL Publishing Services, Tiverton
Printed and bound in England by SRP Ltd, Exeter

Contents

POLLY CLARK

Reconciliation

It's my first day. I cycled here in my trainers and I have forgotten my shoes. It's a building like a pile of cardboard boxes. My trainers definitely will look weird with my skirt, so I'll tell them that my feet hurt and it will be better – if they don't mind – if I walk in bare feet. I hurt my feet... mountaineering, I'll say.

It's cold and raining. A thirty foot Christmas tree draped in lights rears in front of the main entrance, but it doesn't cheer the place up.

Mountaineering? asks the fat girl in personnel doubtfully. Yes, I say, in Scotland. I don't elaborate.

I'm posted on the third floor: credit control. It's a bunker in hazardous beige. The soles of my feel toil across the industrial carpet. The desks are lined up like cars in a jam, each with a driver who never looks up. There's no sound except the clicking of computer keys and my feet, flailing across the carpet. Here and there, tinsel has been wrapped around the edges of desks and hung around whatever is on the wall: a fire extinguisher, a health and safety notice. I warm up a little.

I'm wearing the clothes I slept in. It saved me 20 minutes this morning and meant I could sleep a little longer. My outfit is a skirt and lycra top so there's no creasing, so who would know? My brilliant time-saving idea of dry-washing my hair is less successful. I sprinkled talc on my scalp and rubbed it in as I am sure I read somewhere, then attempted to brush it out, but it has clumped at the roots and I know I look as if I have

1

been renovating a house and my head has not recovered from bringing down the ceiling.

But I am here, which is pretty good. I put my chin up a little as I advance with the fat girl from personnel up to my manager's desk.

His name is Vernon. He looks like a turtle. More specifically he looks like a turtle without its carapace which gives him a rather exposed and nervous air. When he turns his head his neck stretches and crinkles like a rhino in latex. I bite my lip as I reach the desk. I try to smile. His arms in his shiny blue shirt are curved protectively around his papers, as if all of us, being human, are prone to cheating.

His eyes flick about the room, an alarmed chameleon. 'Laura,' he says. 'What are you doing here?'

'Do you two know each other?'

Vernon sighs. 'This is my wife, Laura.'

'Oh,' says the fat girl. I slide one foot over the other.

'Forget your shoes?' Vernon says softly. I don't know if I reply, if I do it is in a whisper. I hope he realises how much planning, thought, how much *normality* it took for me to be here today. I hope he understands what it means, the seriousness with which I take him, and us. I increase my smile. You might say I *flash him a smile*. It says, 'Aren't you glad to see how much I wanted to see you again?'

'So... Is this okay then Mr Pringle? Laura is your temp.'

Ah. Vernon nods wisely. I am triumphant. I know every line of that face. That face has watched over me, that face has known me at my best. The women lift their heads from their gridlock and stare. This is something a bit thrilling – Mr Pringle's wife.

'Yes, it's fine,' Vernon says. Fat girl edges away, flapping clumpy lashes. 'I'll call to see how you're getting on later.'

Vernon's lips curl, as if each one individually is considering me. There is a silence. 'So...' says Vernon.

We regard each other over months of frozen silence. Not from me I might add. I'm a talker, a communicator. It was always what was special about Vernon and me, the talk, the chatting. We began our relationship – half my life ago – in a bar, and those were our best times, telling each other the truth of our lives in the warm light. I might be defective in every other way, defective enough to mean that I must be divorced, defective enough to mean that silence is actually my lot, but it doesn't mean it comes naturally to me. News and questions bubble up in my throat, but I cannot speak. He looks so like my husband, and yet... How has he managed to remain himself, to become – dare I say it – *even more* himself, with not even a scar and even a brand new blue shirt?

He leans in towards me conspiratorially. I feel his breath ruffle the molecules around my face. 'How are you on reconciliations, Laura?'

Warmth floods me to my fingertips. A hand lifts to my hair. 'I don't know,' I grin.

'Well we'd better get you a desk.' He stands, light rocketing off him. I don't say this lightly (how can these people stand the merciless striplights?), he really is vast in the scraps of their shadows. His thick shoulders shift like branches in a gale. I follow him. His walk, just as I remember, is heavier on the left than the right. I catch him, I hiss, 'What do you think about this then? You and me, you and me in a place like this?' My voice becomes a fluttering laugh.

'Well it is a turn-up, yes,' he says. We have arrived at a desk in the corner. It is completely bare, made of gleaming plastic. It overlooks the parking lot where thousands of cars all point the same way. I feel giddy, anything is possible now. Vernon's shirt feels harsh and cheap in my fingers. 'I've grown some onions in the garden, and I had an interview last week.' I say. These are both, technically, lies, but could be true.

'Good,' he says, with familiar gentleness. We sit on opposite sides of the desk, as if he were my lawyer and I were about to tell him everything. I lean on my elbows smiling conspiratorially.

'Laura, you're all right?' he asks.

I am irritated by this mannerism of his that has not changed, his way of presenting a question as a statement with an overwhelmingly positive bias, so that to dispute it seems an unbearable effort, not to say churlish, given his kindness and concern.

'Yes?' he repeats.

'Of course,' I say, caught out even as I see myself being caught out.

He nods, and I notice (who could not?) a striking weariness around his eyes. 'Janny?' he calls to a smooth blonde head bobbing behind a computer terminal. A young face bends round, eyes us both innocently.

'Can you pass me a yellow highlighter?' Janny is perfectly matte. The highlighter looks plain-Jane in her manicured hand. Her lipstick is arterial red. I am overcome with such fierce hatred for her that I know it's the truth.

Vernon lays two long printouts in front of me. They spill down my lap and onto the floor. There is a long column of numbers on each.

'What you have to do,' he says, regarding me carefully, 'is mark the figures which are the same on each sheet. So –' his hand marks 44.61 on one page and 44.61 a few numbers down on page two.

'Oh,' I say. I take the highlighter from him. 'What if I can't find a matching number on the other sheet?'

'Then it remains unreconciled.' He gets up to go. 'Pass it to Janny when you're done.' The scent of him scatters, falling all over me unbearably. 'Don't leave me,' I say, but like almost everything I say it falters at my lips. He observes me, looks as if he too might say something. *I am your wife. That is everything that I am. Help me*, I nearly say. But we don't say anything. I watch him leave and do not move.

My eyes fall on the numbers. The columns are perfect, right aligned, their utter randomness and uniformity clutches my brain. I see 418.80, I gasp at the symmetry at its heart, its left-heaviness, the roundedness of the right hand side. I scan the other column and there is an unexpected thrill when 418.80 sneakily appears somewhere around my knees. I highlight the pair. My success glows.

Where is Vernon? I do not know. For a fragment of a minute I do not ask myself the question.

What about 22.48 and 22.49 – do they belong to each other? After all, they are so nearly the same. But then, 22.48 presents itself, collects its perfect partner and 22.49 remains unreconciled. In this way minutes pass, minutes that become over an hour. At last I can say that the figures left on my sheet have no home, no partner: spinsterish they sit in tidy superfluity until Janny appears in front of me and says, 'Have you finished there? Shall I take it?' She smiles and her teeth are short and polished. I fancy I can see my reflection in them, cut in half.

'Where is Vernon?' I ask. I ask the question from a point of disadvantage. My head is level with her belly. She seems perfectly able to place an immaculate hand on my head and issue a blessing. Under the desk I rub one foot over the other.

'Mr Pringle has a meeting,' says Janny. 'He'll be out for most of the day. He asked me to tell you what to do next.'

'Oh,' I say.

'How did you find the reconciliation?' She casts a sparkling eye over my highlighting.

'What happens to the numbers that don't get matched?'

'They remain unreconciled.'

'But what *happens*?'

Janny frowns slightly. 'Well we find out where they have come from. We trace them back. Find an explanation.'

'Oh.'

'You seem to have done very well here.' The paper squeaks and fights in her hands.

'Can I do the finding out? I mean I'd like to find out why 22.49 so narrowly missed being 22.48…'

'It's more complicated… you have to look through the invoices. Go right back to the beginning.' She looks at me doubtfully. 'Do you have accounting experience?'

'Oh yes. I used to… I used to keep the books for my mountaineering club.' I grin again. Where is Vernon? Why can't he see this, my robust best?

'Well, if you like. We can see how you get on. All the paperwork is in the files beside Mr Pringle's desk. You could pop yourself there while he's out.' Does she realise what she has given me? Studying her for a second, I think she does and her eyes flicker away.

'OK,' I say casually, and can hardly stop myself from skipping to my husband's desk. I settle myself carefully, smiling proprietorially. I check the drawers, find a dusty miscellany of pens, old labels, post-it notes. When I glance up I meet eyes that are trying not to stare. Janny, love of my love – I hold back from gripping her expensive delicately perfumed sweater – lays the printouts I have just finished on the desk. 'Behind you in the cabinet are the invoices, in order by company. Go through each one and see if any of the figures you can't reconcile are on them. Give me a shout when you find one.'

'I will,' I say.

Outside the day is darkening already. I remember the cold of my flat. I don't want to go back there. I don't ever want to go back there. My new life is in filing. I have a *filing personality*. Where files might make another person depressed, queasy even, I realise that in files are the *answers*. I turn to the filing cabinet behind me. I want to find out how 22.49 should have come into being, how it came to have that little bit of excess, that made it unreconcilable. I want its story. When I know its story I can let it go.

'Laura?'

'Yes?' I look up from my work. I have not looked up for a very long time. For a while my forehead was almost resting on the desk. My eyes are heavy.

'How are you getting on?' Janny has appeared, like a sweetly evil nun.

'I can't find it. I've searched every invoice. I can't find it.'

'You've spent all afternoon on 22.49?'

'Of course.'

I turn back to the last sheet in my current handful. And when I move my wrist, I can't believe it, it's there – ninth figure down on an invoice for small car parts from MacGregor's. Six pipe caps, ex VAT and delivery: 22.49! Not lost, only mislaid!

'There it is!' I screech.

I feel Vernon's hand on my shoulder, and an enormous weariness settles on me. 'I found it,' I say.

'Well done, Laura,' says Vernon. His hand through my top is warm.

Janny is standing close to me. I can smell her careful cleanliness, and I don't think I ever longed to be someone so much as I long to be her.

'Laura has worked very hard today. I think she has done very well,' she says.

There is a long silence. I realise that people are standing and putting on their coats, though my head is bowed and my eyes are closed. The movement of someone near me dislodges some tinsel which drifts and crashes softly over my feet.

'Do you want to come back tomorrow?' says Vernon. I look up. I think of my cold house. I remember my old life. It included this person, this person before me in a cheap blue shirt. I cannot make sense of it. I need help to make sense of it.

'Please,' I say. 'Please.'

Janny and Mr Pringle look at each other. Janny says crisply, 'Excellent.'

'Remember your shoes,' says Vernon, his smile rolling out slowly.

I look back as I leave. There is a glass of water with a sprig of holly in it on my desk. The fat girl from personnel is in the lift as I go down. 'OK Laura?'

'OK,' I say.

It is black outside, and freezing. I am shivering in seconds as I hunt for my bike. The dark shuts me in like a lid. Looking forward, I see the road has the gawky beauty of a list of numbers unfurling. I stop and I get on my knees by the side of the road. I take my time, though it is desperately cold. I examine the sparkling surface of the road for the explanation, which I know now with a wonderful warm certainty is there.

Lucille

Every day Gabriel would go to Wimbledon Common in order to trap birds and small animals such as rabbits for Lucille. He hated doing this, being an animal lover in the English way, and it sometimes distressed him to tears to carry their bodies home, feeling their warmth against his body through the bag he kept for the purpose. When he got home he would lay them out on a tray and leave the room while Lucille ate them. He wished that she would eat the same food as him, as she had done before they were married, but Lucille refused. Gabriel ate his supper alone in the kitchen, listened at the living room door until there was no sound then he took her tray away and washed up. Sometimes they would watch television together in the evenings, but mostly Gabriel went to work in the small cupboard space he had cleared out for himself. He worked as a freelance accountant, but was trying to write his autobiography and in the evenings it was the autobiography he pondered over, without ever actually writing anything.

Mostly Lucille liked to sleep during the day, waking up around dusk. She liked to occupy the corner of the living room furthest from the window. She had lately begun to keep the curtains drawn all the time, and so the room was very dark, but he knew where everything was and so didn't bump into things much. If he wanted light he could go out into the kitchen which was south-facing with large windows. There was the garden too, with a patio and chairs where he could get some fresh air, and beyond the house the buzz and bustle of the main street with its collection of shops, where he could wander and fill himself up with the sounds of life.

★★

Over the years, Gabriel's clients had drifted away as Lucille demanded more and more time. His one remaining client was Rayner, who had an unshakeable belief in his genius with numbers. A friendship had developed between them, never outwardly acknowledged, but manifested in Rayner's refusal to find a more efficient accountant and Gabriel's devotion of vast amounts of unpaid time to the complexities of Rayner's finances.

Rayner's skin was the colour of baby mice and he had an energetic disinterest in his own money. At tax return time, or indeed at any other time, he would ask Gabriel to his house to 'crunch the numbers' with him. He would appear attentive and ask to have everything explained, but shortly afterwards his wife Mai would produce an enormous lunch and somehow the discussion would never quite get underway. At every meeting Gabriel tried to alert Rayner to the importance of getting his financial affairs sorted, but Rayner waved it aside. 'I'm a stupendous judge of character, Gaby, and I know you'll make it clear it to me eventually.'

One day Rayner decided to transfer some of the accounting discussions to his club. 'How about it Gaby? We can relax, really get to grips with the figures.' Despite himself, Gabriel found the prospect quite exciting. In seconds the files were packed up and Rayner was driving them to the club.

Gabriel had never been in a place like it. It was full of men like Rayner, some much younger, who seemed to be journalists or perhaps novelists. The club had a rich, edgy air which Gabriel liked. It was a revelation to him. Drinks were brought round by girls who were very pretty and smiled at him warmly. Gabriel found it difficult to concentrate on the matter of allowable expenses under the circumstances, but

Rayner seemed unconcerned. Within minutes they had a gathering round them of his friends. Gabriel thought of Lucille and how probably he should get back but then Rayner leaned over and said to him, 'A man should never have to be lonely, Gabriel. It's not good.'

Gabriel said, 'No, I'm sure not.' A drink appeared in his hand, and then another. And then a girl sat beside him. She had a perfect button nose and thick black hair and she asked Gabriel lots of questions about himself and when he told her about his work as an accountant she didn't seem bored at all, and when he told her about his dream of writing his autobiography she seemed genuinely fascinated. Then at one point, when he was telling her how he was thinking of beginning his autobiography at the present moment and working backwards, she leaned forward and kissed him.

Gabriel felt a terrible plummet of longing, which then became a wave of homesickness which he thought might drown him. 'Rayner, I have to go,' he said. 'I'm very sorry,' he said to the girl, squeezing her hand.

All the way home he was in a sweat of guilt, and at the same time he felt alive in a way he had not ever felt. He could still feel the girl's warmth against him, the touch of her on his mouth. When he got home, he heard Lucille restless in her usual place. He crept past the door and into the bed. He licked his lips in the darkness, mouthed *I'm home*.

★★

One day soon after this Gabriel arrived home from seeing Rayner, feeling quite pleased with himself as he had saved him quite a large slice of tax. Rayner had given him a bottle of rather good whiskey as a thank you (being unable to persuade him to go to the club). He would have liked to share the news with Lucille, but it was not a good time for her: she was fast asleep in her corner of the living room. When they were first married she had occupied the armchair that had been his mother's but as time went on she found it more comfortable to crouch in the corner of the room.

It was a sunny day, and Gabriel decided that he would have a small celebratory whiskey before his usual 6pm watershed. The whiskey was extremely good stuff, more than thirty years old, and Gabriel was rather excited as he unscrewed the cap on the bottle and opened the cupboard to get out one of the crystal whiskey glasses.

Being very English and very reserved, Gabriel was not prone to screaming, but when he saw the dead body of the small dog, wrapped in glossy threads of silk and hidden amongst the glasses, he whimpered. He could not tell what kind of dog it was, but it was the size of a spaniel, and he could see its outline through the layers of silk. He could see its mouth pressed open, and the bump of its eyes. Its legs and tail had been bent against its body to make a neat package.

As he was recovering himself, he heard Lucille behind him.

'What's this?' he whispered.

She said nothing and hunched herself together anxiously.

'But it's a *dog*, Lucille. What is it doing here?'

Lucille did not like persistent questioning. 'It was a stray dog. It didn't look well. I think it was very old.'

'And?'

'I thought I might get hungry,' she said irritably.

Gabriel took a deep breath. 'You can't keep a thing like this. We'll have to throw it away, Lucille. I'm sorry.'

Lucille's eyes brimmed with tears. 'But it took me ages to wrap it up. And it would have died anyway,' she pleaded. But this was a matter where Gabriel felt quite firm and did not think that marital compromise was possible. Bracing himself against the retch of disgust which enveloped him he picked up the parcel. It felt curiously dry and strongly wrapped, and was very stiff and heavy. Gabriel considered for several minutes what was the best way to get rid of it, so that the neighbours wouldn't see anything. He put it in a bin bag, piled on top some cans and a packet of Shreddies and put it in the dustbin outside the front door, pressing the lid down firmly. Lucille watched him mournfully from the kitchen and crept back into the living room.

That evening Lucille did not eat the rabbit Gabriel had caught for her, nor did she utter a word for a full day afterwards. Every look she gave him was full of reproach, which made him feel desperately guilty. He lay awake all night wondering what he could do to make it up to her.

★★

The flower shop on the main road was called Buttercups and contained so many flowers it was quite difficult to make out the counter. Gabriel realized that he had never set foot inside, in over a decade of walking past it almost every day. The young woman behind the counter had a blonde ponytail and wore an overall covered in roses. She gave a small smile that almost reached her eyes.

'I'd like some flowers please,' Gabriel managed finally.

'Well you've come to the right place. Browse away.'

Gabriel didn't move, overwhelmed by the sheer number of flowers. The woman watched him with a puzzled expression.

'Are they for your wife?'

'Yes.'

'What kind of flowers does she like?'

Gabriel realized at this that Lucille had no interest in flowers whatsoever. The only interest she had ever exhibited in them was to pick bees from the centre of the roses in his sister's garden and chew them noisily. He stared at the shop assistant not knowing quite what to do next.

'OK then… what are the flowers for? Is it an anniversary? Or are you in the dog house?' The smile, while not increasing at all, managed to look very sympathetic.

'Er... yes, that. The dog house. Yes, that's it, the dog house.'

'Ah well, in that case.' The girl came out from behind the counter and began busying herself among the buckets. 'Let me see... lilies, all women love lilies. They are the thoughtful flowers.' She was talking mostly to herself. Gabriel watched her in silence, as her hands splashed among the stems.

'How badly are you in the dog house?'

'Oh... er, pretty bad.' Gabriel wanted her to keep moving among the flowers. He was fascinated. She chose and lifted the flowers deftly with her left hand, slipping them into a deep pocket on the right side of her overall. As she did so, she seemed to dislodge the fragrance of the flowers. The smell of flowers filled his head and seemed to fill the whole world.

The girl was back behind the counter, unrolling a long strip of tissue paper from a roll, tearing it off with a powerful flick of her wrist. She lifted the stems one by one and laid them on the paper, her head tilted in concentration. The arrangement was quite complicated, interleaved with pretty fern-like stems, and she pursued the task in silence, finally rolling the paper around the stems with another seamless action. Then she stood the bouquet in a hoop behind the counter while she unraveled some ribbon from another reel and sliced it on a blade. She wrapped it round the bouquet, then looked up at him. 'Just need you to hold this end,' she said, holding out a piece of ribbon. Gabriel held the ribbon between finger and thumb, trying to concentrate. She pulled the fastening taut, took the piece from him, wrapped it around the flowers again and now when he looked, the bouquet was tied with a perfect pink velvet bow.

'If that doesn't get you out of trouble, I don't know what will,' said the girl. She took his money and wiped her hand on her overall before giving him his change. 'Good luck!'

Gabriel paused for a moment as he took the bouquet, waiting to see if the smile would grow. It remained maddeningly constant.

'What's your name?' he blurted.

Her head tilted ever so slightly to one side. 'Clara.'

'That's a nice name.' he said. 'I've never been in here before, even though... even though I've lived round the corner for years.'

There wasn't much Clara could add to this. She nodded encouragingly. 'Sometimes it takes a while for the right moment for flowers to come,' she said.

'Yes. Yes, absolutely. The right moment for flowers has come!' Briefly Clara's soft smile was eclipsed by the grin that covered Gabriel's face at this exchange. He waved happily and stepped out of the shop with the armful of flowers into the busy street that smelled of diesel and dust.

When he had gone, Clara thought of the man, and how funny he was. *Imagine*, she thought. *Not even knowing what flowers your wife likes!* She pictured him returning to his house and his wife's delighted face (because she would be delighted – no one could fail to be so with such a bunch of flowers). She both liked and did not like to imagine this scene. She liked it because her flowers would make someone happy, as flowers, properly arranged, in the right hands will do. And she did not like it because it reminded her that she had no existence beyond this roomful of flowers, and the only contact she had with people was the pleasure that came from what her hands had arranged. Thinking of this made her tired. She closed up the shop and went to have a nap on her tiny bed in the back room.

★★

'Darling, I have a present for you!' Gabriel called as he opened the door. As he did so he was almost certain that he heard a scraping and a rustling sound. The living room door seemed to click shut just as he stepped into the hall.

'Lucille?' he called.

There was no reply. He opened the living room door and

everything was still. He switched on the light and Lucille flinched in her corner. Her eyes were wide and bright, and fixed on him innocently.

'I brought you these,' he said holding out the flowers. 'I wanted to say sorry.'

'OK,' said Lucille, not moving.

'Do you like them?'

'Yes. Maybe you'd better put them in water.'

'Good idea. I think we have a vase somewhere.'

While he was in the kitchen, Gabriel heard more scraping and rustling from the living room. He reappeared in the doorway to find Lucille perched on the sofa. She looked at him in alarm.

'Lucille? What's wrong?' he asked.

'Nothing,' she said quickly.

'Why are you on the sofa then? You never sit on the sofa.'

'Fancied a change,' she replied uncertainly.

'What's that?' Gabriel pointed at something sticking out from behind the sofa cushion.

'Nothing.'

'It's not nothing, darling. I can see it.' Gabriel went over and removed the sofa cushion. The silky parcel of another dog slid onto the floor. Gabriel squealed involuntarily and stepped back. 'Dear God! Lucille!'

They stared at one another. Outside the window children's voices grew and died away. 'Why are you doing this?' said Gabriel in a voice not much above a whisper. 'Why are you doing this?'

Lucille said nothing, crept down from the sofa and pressed herself into a ball in her usual corner. Gabriel picked up the parcel. It was still slightly warm. This time he wrapped it in newspaper before laying it in the bottom of a thick black bin bag and pressing it to the bottom of the dustbin outside.

**

It seemed to Gabriel, as he struggled with the first line of his autobiography, that what was needed was something that both he and Lucille could love. That would bring this terrible stasis to an end, and surely with something to love, Lucille would no longer need to exhibit this strange behaviour. He paused after the phrase *The evening is beautiful*, and flushed with excitement at this revelation. Somewhere in the bin was the local paper. He fished it out and went to the classifieds. With his red accounting pen he circled three advertisements.

The next morning Clara was setting the buckets on the pavement outside the shop when she saw Gabriel drive past. Something made her look up, and there it was: the shiny blue Golf pausing at the crossing outside the shop. Gabriel had his sleeves drawn up: already it was a warm day. The car disappeared slowly into the glut of traffic. She continued stacking her buckets, and adjusted the awning to give just the right amount of shade.

★★

It was quite difficult to hold the cardboard box still. It jiggled and bounced. Whines and snuffles came from inside. Smiling to himself, Gabriel wedged the box firmly under his arm as he locked the car door. The house was quiet. Whistling, he called Lucille's name and opened the living room door.

'Darling?'

He switched on the light. Lucille ventured out of her corner slightly. The electric light cast a towering shadow of her across the far wall. Gabriel sat down on the sofa, the box at his feet.

'I got us something,' he said. 'Something of our very own.'

Lucille brightened, moved a little closer to the box. Her shadow moved with her and expanded across the wall. Gabriel opened the box and lifted out a tiny gold puppy. It wriggled in his hands, snorting and yapping excitedly. He laid it down on the floor between them.

'I thought we could call him George. Remember my uncle George? The one who was killed in the war? He had bright gold hair this colour. What do you think?'

Lucille said nothing. Her eyes were fixed on the tiny creature who was chasing his tail, slipping on the wooden floor, barking a tiny bark. He ran round the box, then darted towards Lucille, slipping in and out of her legs, galloping back towards Gabriel. Lucille moved backwards a little and regarded the creature nervously.

'He doesn't bite,' said Gabriel. 'I specifically asked about that. He's a Labrador. He'll be great fun.'

Gabriel's attention was fixed on the puppy. He held out his fingers to it, and George licked them. 'Good boy!' Gabriel said. He did not see Lucille, shrunken now beneath her shadow, staring at him. If he had looked at her, he would have seen, for the first time since they had married, a new expression in her eyes. It was there only for a moment before she resumed watching the antics of the puppy. It was a look, quite definitely, of fear.

★★

Rayner had a summer party in his garden, to which of course Gabriel was invited. He asked if he could bring George. 'Of course!' boomed Rayner. 'Although I don't want him impregnating Mai's Dachshund Celia. And she's a terrible flirt, so be warned.'

'Oh George is still very young,' said Gabriel.

'And will you be bringing your, er…'

'Lucille? No, it will just be me and George.'

He clipped George's lead to his shiny new collar and gave him a biscuit for no reason other than George was a lovely little creature. He called to Lucille, but there was no answer. He pushed open the living room door and found it impossible to open fully due to the silk curtain woven firmly behind it.

'I'm off, darling. Back later,' said Gabriel, breaking the curtain as far as he could. Threads dropped all over him. A whole skein settled across his back. He could just see Lucille's shape hunched in the darkness. She was sleeping, so he closed the door and set off. The weaving was a new development. He did not know what it meant.

★★

Rayner's wife nudged him, spilling champagne down his blazer. 'Who is that man?' she asked, indicating a thin and shambling person emerging up the drive with a tiny dog leaping around at the end of a lead. As he got closer, it became apparent that he was covered in dust and threads of some sort of gossamer-like material, of which he seemed completely unaware.

'Good God. It's Gabriel.' said Rayner. 'What's happened to him? Gabriel! How lovely of you to come.'

'My pleasure,' said Gabriel happily. Mai stared at him. She was not pleased to have him there at all. Later she would complain to Rayner, 'But he was covered in things. He is thin and ill. He is not a hygienic person!' George was yapping excitedly. 'He'll calm down,' Gabriel said, taking a biscuit from his pocket and giving it to the dog.

'Come and have a drink and a chat indoors,' said Rayner. 'Mai – the Beechings have arrived, would you get them a drink?'

In his study, Rayner cleared his throat from behind his desk. 'Gabriel,' he began, 'how are things? I mean, really.'

Gabriel looked startled. 'Oh fine. You know.'

'You know if you want to get away for a few days or anything, you can always come here.' Rayner said this forcefully.

Gabriel looked at Rayner in some confusion. 'Get away for a few days? That's very kind, but I have a lot of work and so on...' He pulled a thread of silk from his face where it was tickling his eyelid and wiped it on his sweater. George wheeled round at the end of his lead and licked the lace of Gabriel's right shoe. Gabriel laughed, his face shining with delight.

Rayner watched his friend as he stroked the dog. He filled a glass and held it out to Gabriel, in the manner of someone who knows there is absolutely nothing to be done.

★★

Clara found herself following the man she thought of as the Funny Man. She saw him walk past the shop, and she darted to the window just in time to see him disappear into the pet shop. She waited until he emerged with a carrier bag awkward with tins, and let him walk back past the shop. Then she flipped the sign to *Closed* and slipped out after him.

He walked quickly, head down, along two streets, packed with parked cars and overspilling shrubs, glancing up briefly to check the traffic as he crossed. She ducked behind a car as he paused outside a house and pulled his keys out of his pocket. She waited until he went inside, then unable to stop herself she crept up towards the house.

The curtains were tightly drawn. She stood opposite the house and watched it. The sensible part of her, the part that had devised a business plan for her little shop and got the loans and made the drudgery of flowers into a thriving business, asked her repeatedly, *What are you doing? You do not even know him. The man has a wife he buys flowers for.* And the part of her that was lonely, that could not sleep for its loneliness kept her rooted to the spot.

Nothing was happening. She sat on the kerb opposite the house and waited. She imagined Mrs Funny Man regarding her sweetly errant husband as she busied herself around the house. She wondered what he had done to merit the flower purchase. She imagined it could not be so serious. Perhaps they were sat out in the garden now sharing a glass of wine. Or perhaps their reunion had spilled over into a whole new falling in love. Perhaps at this moment they were lying together in bed.

The afternoon was clouding over and a wind was picking up. A crisp packet bounced down the middle of the street, doing a series of near perfect cartwheels. The door to the flat opened. Clara froze, edged behind a car.

Gabriel appeared on the doorstep, carrying in his arms a black dustbin liner. He was clutching it tightly to his chest and his head was bowed. Rain was beginning to fall. Gabriel stood on the step for a long time, appearing not to know whether to set the bag down or to walk out of the house completely.

Clara began to walk towards him, with no idea of what she would say. Perhaps she would just enquire after the flowers, had they been all he hoped for? As she approached Gabriel lifted the lid of the dustbin and pressed the package into it. She glimpsed that it was something small.

Above her a streetlight flickered into life. Caught in its beam, Clara began to cry. She was envious of the domestic scene: a husband taking out the rubbish, and somewhere back inside the house perhaps, a wife calling him. Gabriel blinked in her direction for a moment, slowly recognizing her. He did not seem surprised that she was there. He smiled at her, as if to be crying under a streetlight in the rain was really the most normal thing in the world. Then he turned and went back into the house, closing the door behind him.

A Season in Hell

One evening I took beauty in my arms – Arthur Rimbaud

This morning is a bad one. There is a fog in my head. My wife, Louise, is shaking the family sized container of Nurofen which is the household substitute for breakfast. When I go to my study to begin my morning's work – the eternal attempt to write a decent poem – there is Arthur, in his white shirt and his perfect black trousers, his legs crossed and a pair of soft black slipper shoes on his feet. I say nothing. I go to my computer. He puts down the book he is skimming disinterestedly and puts his hands behind his head, regarding me with amusement from beneath his cloud of dark hair.

I have a dedication for the poem: *To Louise, again and forever*, but the poem won't follow. It is something she said last night as we lay side by side, not unfriendly but so far from touching that to have been strangers would have brought more possibilities to the situation. She said, 'I want to die before you.'

I was not shocked by this. It seems these days that nothing really shocks me: not that that means I am exactly prepared for such a remark.

'Why?' I asked.

'Because everything will come out. It will be a humiliation for me.' She went very quiet and turned away. I wanted to touch her shoulder in a reassuring way, but sleep overwhelmed me. In the morning we did not refer to it, each

23

of us waiting for the small increments of the day to wear it away, to erode it to the point where it was just something else we said.

'Once, if my memory serves me well, my life was a banquet where every heart revealed itself, where every wine flowed,' I say with a small protesting smile, sitting now at the computer with my back to Arthur. It is a game I play with him. It provokes him because often he cannot remember his own lines, and often he hates them anyway.

'One evening I took Beauty in my arms,' he says, close behind me, so that I can feel his breath on my neck, deciding that today he will play. He likes to bother me when I begin my work. He likes to look around the room and peer over my shoulder. Of course it is a distraction, a delicious distraction.

The poem I am struggling over is one I have been asked to write about the refurbishment of some council offices in Sheffield. The way to approach these dry, dreadful commissions is to try desperately not to think of the money and to find a personal angle. They're introducing some plywood circular affair in the manner of Brussels, so that everyone is facing everyone else. It's the end of adversarial politics, said the commission letter. *The adversary is beside me now*, I begin. I began this several days ago.

'I want to perish chewing on their gun butts. I have called for plagues, to suffocate in sand and blood,' adds Arthur, poisonously. He yawns and slumps back in the chair. He is in his mid-thirties, poetry bores him. Some days I bore him too and these are extremely bad days when he prowls around the study and the house, refusing to leave but refusing also to let me get on. Some days I have to say that I hate Arthur, that Arthur seems intent on ruining my life, by simply filling it up with himself so that I can't think and I can't write. But today, when he slumps back in the armchair and looks at me, dark and triumphant, the mischievous invitation playing around his eyes, I am swamped with such a feeling of delight that I feel that writing this poem is possible and there will be more after it, more and more, as long as he stays with me and walks near me as I work, almost touching me.

**

Arthur tells me again as I unlock my office at the university what a sell-out and a loser I am. He does not understand that the twenty-first century poet must *work*. I tried to explain that no one gives a damn about poems, that actually poems are pointless fripperies to most of the world even if you feel it's your life to write them. The last time we had this conversation, with him draped louchely over the back of the office chair normally reserved for students, he spat at me. It missed my shoe by about half an inch. 'Why didn't you just stop?' he asks. 'Why end up here, like this, shut in this fucking coffin, doing nothing of any importance. Is this what you hoped for?'

Today I turn away from him, try to shut him out. I can feel him staring at me, penetratingly. My hands tremble as I fumble through my papers. Between the pile of student poems on my desk (small with flickers of promise) and the pile of student novel chapters (towering and dull) is a small wrapped object. When I unwrap it carefully I see that it is a first edition of my very first book of poems.

It is a small hardback book, pale blue, the cover faded now and torn at the corners. On the cover is an etching of a deer emerging from a wood, and the title is printed above it simply in black *This is the Last*. I half-smile to myself: it was a terrible mistake of a title, but oh, when I open the book and leaf through, the pages tears burn at the back of my throat. Poems more than forty years old, that I have not even thought about in a decade leap out at me. I hold the book out to Arthur. *See*, I hiss. *I can do it. This is a good book. This is a bloody good book*.

He tilts his head, looks at me gorgeously. 'My point precisely.'

'Fuck off,' I say. 'Haven't you got anything better to do with your day than to ruin mine?' I lay the book gently on the pile of poems. Perhaps whoever left it there will make themselves known. Arthur, with one of his more self-satisfied smiles wanders out of the room.

In the five minutes before tutorials begin I make a note of the following: that the sun is blind–white and completely savage today; that this morning Louise's hair had a particular coarseness, a weariness about it; and that there is a meeting to discuss the development of this writing course at 2pm next Thursday. *Must* talk to the Chair.

There is a knock on the door. 'Come in! Caroline?'

My first student of the morning. She is the very tall and fragile-looking girlfriend of Jordach, my favourite student. Today she wears a tight cream polo neck and a skirt which is not short but is tight. In seminars she always sits in a chair directly in my line of view, and she usually has her head in her hands, her eyes fixed on me.

'Hello, how are you this morning?' I say with a glittering smile. I lift the book from the pile and move it to one side to sift for her poems. This is, generally, the most tiring part of my working day.

'Do you like it?' she interrupts, nodding towards the book.

'You got this for me?' I stare at her. 'Even I haven't got one! How on earth did you find it?'

'Hay-on-Wye. Tucked away in a little shop. I wanted it for myself, but I thought you might like to have it.'

I am touched. 'Thank you,' I manage. I wonder for a fraction of a second what she sees when she looks at me. Does she see something like the young man on the back of the book? Does she see anything approximating what is really here, now?

'Your poems,' I say. I turn to the thin sheaf of poems, which I now remember sadly were rather flat, rather narcissistic. 'I was struck by a lot of the images. Can you tell

26

me more about the image of the lawn as an asylum in this first poem?'

'Actually Professor, there is something else I need to tell you.'

'Oh?'

Caroline looks desperately uncomfortable. Her face is flushed and she has trouble meeting my eye. 'What is it?' I ask, suddenly concerned.

'I'm leaving the course. I thought… I thought I was a poet, and then I got on the course and I realised that I am not. *You* are a poet.'

'But these poems are good –' I begin, as begin I must.

'Well perhaps they are all right,' she says thoughtfully. 'But all right is not good enough, is it? And I don't think they will ever be better than that. Anyway, I'm not sad about it. I'm probably going to do a journalism course or something. I haven't decided. I just didn't want you to think that it was your fault. I've understood this because of you.'

I sit back a moment, look at her anew. 'But are you sure? How can you be sure?'

'I'm sure.'

'What does Jordach have to say about it?'

'I don't think it is really anything to do with him.' She looks at me steadily.

In different guises Caroline has come to me many times over the years. Dozens and dozens of fresh faced girls who have confused poetry with love, and their teacher with poetry itself. But it never palls, the thrill of a beautiful woman sitting in silence with me like this. Finally she breaks it.

'Are you coming to the party tonight?' she says brightly.

'I'll call in perhaps,' I say.

★★

The student party in general is a ghastly business. But my students expect me to go and I don't like to disappoint. I wear: blue linen jacket, faint pink shirt with Japanese collar (looks like it got washed with something red that bled, but actually is French and very expensive); long black trousers and my black boots with their neat heel. A girl said to me not so long ago, *you're in tremendous shape aren't you?* as I crossed the hotel bedroom. I remember those words as I observe the image in the guest-house mirror. I was a beautiful boy, Arthur. A boy as beautiful as you. Arthur is off doing his own thing tonight, thank God. It exhausts me to keep explaining… I can barely hold on to what I keep trying to explain.

The student party is dank and sweaty. I have to admit that as the years go by the students in general are getting rather less attractive. Perhaps it is their corresponding increase in self-obsessed earnestness, their calculated careerism. An exception to this is, of course, Jordach. I warmed to him as soon as we met. His mind is nimble, and he follows cricket as I do. He turns a good line, and he is beautiful. When I say beautiful, I mean like Arthur is beautiful. He is everything a young poet should be. He is a *good thing*.

Tonight Jordach stands in a small crowd, his arm loosely around the waist of Caroline. His leather jacket is draped around her shoulders, and it looks a little small for her. We swap a couple of observations about the Ashes. He seems a little quiet. Caroline is saying nothing. Her gaze is on me, direct and disconcerting.

'Tutorial in the morning,' I remind Jordach. He smiles, but seems distracted. 'I'd better have another drink to brace myself,' he says. Jordach already has a contract with Harper Collins for his first novel. I don't know how much I have helped him, apart from putting in the call of course. The ones who can do it, who can write, do it without me really. I just open the door and they fly off.

Caroline nods shyly and sips from her bottle. Jordach is talking to someone else now and I lean in to her. Her face lights up. 'It's a real shame you're going,' I say. 'Your sort of insight is exactly what makes a good poet.' She smiles and shakes her head, and then reaches secretly under my jacket and strokes my waist.

'I hear they've done a portrait of you,' she says. 'Oils and gilt frame, all that sort of thing.' She's a bit drunk now. The hand stays secretly at my waist, hooked into my belt.

'They have indeed, and hung it in the rare books library. Not a good likeness at all though. He's much better looking and I suspect more talented.'

'I haven't seen it. Only heard the rumours.'

I hold out my keys, one of which is to the rare books library, open by appointment only. 'Would you like to see it for yourself? You could tell me what you think. The *Telegraph* described it as having unexpected poignancy.'

She whispers something to Jordach, hands him his jacket. He begins to reply, but stops. In the corner of my eye I see his hand on her arm, his nails bitten down to his fingertips. It rests there for a moment. Of course there is pleading in that touch. Of course there is.

Giggling we make our way through the corridors to the library. I wonder briefly if the other students – particularly Jordach – noticed me leave with her, but if they have I expect they'll get drunk, forget, get into their own entanglements, and anyway it's all completely innocent and there's something about the way Caroline is moving ahead of me now, her long sleek body oddly graceless, compelling to watch, that pushes out all other thoughts. And then from a doorway Arthur appears, smirking at me, arms folded. 'She's pretty,' he says, looking her up and down, but then he is beside me, so close I can feel the electricity of his skin, the rustle of his shirt. 'I was unkind earlier,' he whispers. 'You know I loved that book. Don't you remember when it came out and we lay out by the Thames that day? It was a wonderful day, wasn't it?'

'Yes it was,' I say.

'Let's stop all this. Let's start again. It's not too late.'

'Later, Arthur,' I say.

'What?' Caroline asks over her shoulder, but I shake my

head, catch up with her, stroke my hand gently across the back of her neck. When I look back, Arthur has gone.

I let us into the library, with its plywood shelves and against the nearest bookshelf which happens to be Renaissance Art, F through K, I gently slip Caroline's sweater over her head and kiss her.

One evening I took Beauty in my arms – Arthur murmurs as I hold her face close to me. Her eagerness is a surprise to me, not that I expected resistance, but it's the sheer vigour of her that takes me aback. I am reminded of the moment when a fish accepts it is caught: there's a wonderful give in the line. It's like the sudden acceleration of a first class car, this wonderful thing, when a woman kisses you back. I close my eyes and find that everything seems to continue without me. Arthur looks up from his book in my study, shakes his head, raises a quizzical eyebrow. The warmth of Caroline's breath and her skin envelop me, and now Arthur has laid down his book, is curled up on the floor sleeping, his hair shining in the thin beam of light through the window.

Some while later we realise that the floor is cold. Caroline shifts from where she lies against my chest and we look up from the floor into the painted eyes of the Professor who gazes from a backdrop of oak panelling.

'It's a good portrait,' says Caroline. The painted Professor is outrageously good-looking. If truth be known I am rather embarrassed by it. He has a head of thick dark hair and an intensity about him. I open my mouth to make a joke about this, but find my mouth full of different words which I have to press my lips together to prevent myself spilling. *Through what crime, by what fault did I deserve my present weakness? You who imagine that animals sob with sorrow, that the sick despair, that the dead have bad dreams, try now to relate my fall and sleep. I can explain myself no better than the beggar with his endless Aves and Pater Nosters.* Caroline kisses me gently on the cheek, a tiny stamp of loneliness and I have to turn away, I have to get up, with suddenly nothing to say.

★★

Sometimes on the journey back to London, crushed between the boozy commuter and the red-faced child, Arthur keeps me company. He reclines, staring out of the window, smiles when I sip my coffee, indicates with a nod that he knows I am fighting the impulse to have something stronger. *Have you thought,* I said to him once, as the evening turned black beyond the glass, *that it is harder simply to live on as oneself? You don't realise, until one day, on a train, or suddenly bunching up in strange pain on the street – that you're weary. Living is an exhausting business, Arthur. You were lucky, just lucky.*

Now that I think of it, he hasn't been with me on the journey for a while now. I don't know why that should be. I miss him. But he'll be there most likely when I get home. I've decided to go home early today: a slight fever, a paralysing hangover and the fact that Jordach didn't show for his tutorial this morning made me decide that enough is enough. *Don't you remember? This is how it goes on. This is how everything gets jumbled, and you start to get afraid.*

★★

Until I reach our street I don't realise quite how early I am. It is only three o'clock. A whole afternoon to myself. My doomed dry poem presses at my eyes. *And history becomes something held together / the adversaries do not know themselves.* The lines slip into my head, half-lodge. I think it will be all right. I have a day or two, and my body feels adored, a peculiarly dirty renewal. Caroline is scrubbed off me, apart from a blonde hair on my overcoat. I pick it off as let myself in.

Our house is a crumbling Edwardian creature, crouched over one of the deepest sections of the Piccadilly Line. We don't hear the trains, but we feel them. Over the years we have become accustomed to the almost constant vibration of the blood that living in this house brings, and cracks have slowly invaded every wall. We joke that the house is mostly held together by the cracks.

Coat on the hook, boots on the stand and into slippers. Up the wooden stairs, my step light because now lines are starting to form; stolen time has set my mind whirring. The house echoing and creaking, the autumn wind shaking the windows we've so resolutely failed to replace. And then – in the pause before my foot touches the top step, an unexpected, sudden sound, that may be wind, that may be something else. I pause on the landing.

The sound comes again, a low moan. Wind, surely. But then the moan becomes a cry. I run up the second flight of stairs, my legs shaking, my hand gripping the banister and half-hauling me up, as though I were someone else, being dragged somewhere I do not want to go.

The bedroom door is firmly closed. I stand before it and listen. And then hear another sound, one that frightens me more. It is a low, agonised cry. I realise it is coming from my own mouth. I throw open the door and see my beautiful, my life-long companion, *my Arthur* leaping from the bed, rushing to hide himself, and beneath him, *oh darling* –

Louise sits up, naked, her mouth pressed open, her red hair falling over her face.

Arthur is climbing into his trousers, his back to me. I realise the telephone is ringing.

With an apologetic flourish Arthur grabs his white shirt and black coat from the floor. He is slightly out of breath, more physical than I have ever seem him. I want to laugh, I want this to be funny. The phone is still ringing.

His face is full of sorrow. 'It's over,' he says. I hold his arm, not understanding for a moment. Then I do understand, I understand completely, the waste of me, and all the air seems to leave my lungs. My hand falls from his arm, and I hear his footsteps going down the stairs. The phone is still ringing.

'Hello?' my mouth says into the receiver.

It is the secretary from the university. 'Professor –'

The front door clicks shut.

'I have some bad news.' the secretary continues. 'Your student, Jordach. I'm terribly sorry to tell you that he died today. It seems… it seems he may have taken his own life.'

★★

My wife completes her funeral outfit with a black velvet pill box hat and a thick veil. Her face is a suggestion of red lips beneath it. She insisted on coming, though she never knew Jordach. I drive in silence, too slowly. Nothing seems to speed the world up today.

The funeral is a packed event. Parked cars jam the roads leading up to the church, whose minute and uneven carpark is also overflowing. People are milling around outside, gathered in dark-clad groups. As we approach the entrance I see faces swollen and tear-stained, young people weeping quietly in corners. *Can there be anything*, I will say in my speech, *can there be anything that redeems the loss of a young man before he becomes what he might have been*?

At the door stand Jordach's mother and father. It must be them: they are the ones who look as though they have been murdered and yet somehow are still alive. His father, from whom Jordach clearly got that pretty face, is wide-eyed and impassive. He does not really see us as he thanks us for coming. His mother, beneath a wide black hat, stares at us all as if we were imposters.

'Thank you so much for agreeing to speak, Professor,' says Mr Jordach. 'I know that my son would have been pleased and proud.'

'Your son had so much potential, Mr Jordach. He really did.' Louise grabs my arm, I think to support me.

When I look back, young people are filling the graveyard and the road beyond, walking slowly, many of them familiar to me. Caroline is approaching, gorgeous in a tight black dress, her blonde hair perfectly coiled on top of her head. She holds my gaze until I look away.

Behind and beyond her, the crowd is growing. Some of the mourners glance my way, but then all of them are swept into this gigantic crowd which cannot possibly fit into a small country church.

I'm sweating. The coffin moves awkwardly up the nave on the shoulders of the young man's brothers and father. Their feet scuff against the stone floor, out of step. The vicar, too young for this himself, struggles to say anything that can offer the slightest comfort. The young man's friends are crying quietly. In a noisy silence I stand and make my way to the pulpit.

The scene before me seems unsteady, the faces looking up at me blurred and dream-like. I look down at my funereal wife, and I press together my own pale hands. *To die when you are young* I begin, catching the eye of Caroline, upright and alert in a middle row. *To die when you are young is the best time to die.*

Mr Jordach's head jerks upright. He is not certain he has heard me right.

The coffin lies directly beneath me. The smell of lilies and roses (coincidentally my favourite flowers) drifts up to me. *He died while he was still beautiful. He died while he was talented. He died before he had been tested – and failed. He died before he could outlive everything that he loved. He will never know this terrible weariness, the weariness we all feel. You know what I am talking about. If you must cry, let it be for yourselves who were not so lucky.*

To a shocked silence I climb down from the pulpit and make my way round the coffin. Here I pause. 'I forgot,' I say. 'I have a reading.' I rest my hands on the coffin lid. *Sometimes in the sky I see endless sandy shores covered in white rejoicing nations. A great golden ship above me flutters many-coloured pennants in the morning breeze. I was the creator of every feast, every triumph, every drama. I tried to invent new flowers, new planets, new flesh, new languages. I thought I had acquired supernatural powers. Ha! I have to bury my imagination and my memories! What an end to a splendid career as an artist and a storyteller!*

I walk down the nave. Jordach's parents are crying in something beyond rage. My wife has her head in her hands and does not look up. As I pass Caroline I catch her eye and nod and she gets up and follows me, pushing through astonished mourners to take my hand. We exit the church, and somewhere beyond it we discover a small outhouse with a door that is not locked. I push it open. It is some sort of storeroom, full of brooms, old shelving, buckets, some with dried paint in them. There is a rusty chandelier thrown on a pile of blankets and I move it to one side and pull Caroline to me. She smiles and runs her hands through my hair as I lift up the tight black dress. If she notices that my lips and my hands are freezing cold she does not say so.

At the Water Cooler

This is how we met: my head was stuck in the office fridge as I tried to decide which of the cartons of milk I could steal from without it being noticed, and I heard a noise behind me. I immediately snapped myself out of the fridge and tried to look casual, and there he was.

He filled himself a cup of water from the water cooler, and then he turned round and stared at me. Not in an *I like you* way. Not in a *you're pretty* way. It was *I've seen you*. He stayed looking at me like that until I left the kitchen. Actually until I ran away. I ran away under the guise of wandering out. I did not look back, in case I should look as horrified as I felt. People passed me in the corridors back to my office, glancing at me as though nothing had happened.

We made it ordinary, we made it as recognizable to other people as we could. So, I could say to my mother, *this is Henry* and he could say to his parents, *here, this is Jill*. We dated, we mingled in groups. And if other people saw what was between us they did not say so. They mistook our need to sneak off into other people's bathrooms at parties, or to spend days together sick from work behind closed curtains as new love or ordinary lust. No one knew it was something we were trying to get rid of, this recognition, this overwhelming need to reach, to *be* the other person. It is no surprise then, perhaps, when you think about it, what happened.

An example of our struggle to be like everyone else? Our trip to Sainsbury's. We liked to speed up at night on

Henry's muddy-black motorbike to the 24-hour superstore. We liked the porn-brightness of the aisles, we liked that there were no shadows anywhere. We loved the people who go shopping at 2am, the sleepless and the lonely, hanging around the spirits or indecisive at the food supplements as they ponder a different life; the shift workers treating it as if it was a busy Saturday, piling the trolley with family packs of everything, and the couples. We were fascinated by the couples most of all. Most of them like us, intoxicated by each other, finding new backdrops for the drama of themselves.

One night we were drifting round the aisles, piling our basket with whatever we fancied: starfruit we didn't know how to cook, Martini we'd never drink in a million years, and five packets of Jaffa Cakes which we would eat in bed, as if we were children. We were congratulating ourselves on our ordinariness: we could participate in the couple-ish conversation about supermarkets, about shopping for two. No one would know from what we said later that when we got to pet food there was no one in that aisle or the next and we were suddenly wrapped around each other, our hands and fingers into each other as if we were a new food.

The cameras caught us of course, and the store detective, corpulent and bespectacled, appeared wearily. 'Do that at home,' he whispered, a fat white hand resting on Henry's shoulder. Henry pulled his face away from mine only reluctantly, turned to smile at the detective, a broad lascivious grin. The detective could not help but smile back, a tentative flutter, come not from recognition, but from a kind of delicious fear.

We did as instructed (always very law-abiding, both of us), leaving the shopping and giggling as we left the store, barely getting home before the fight to be each other resumed on the stairs, or the floor before we reached the bed. I was asked many times, did you love him? *Oh yes*, I always said. *Yes.*

★★

I woke to sunlight singing tunelessly into the bedroom. I pressed my face into the pillow. My mouth hung open like a broken door, and there was a dull throb behind my eyes. I remembered flashes of last night, mainly it involved drinking at a club; at some point early on it dissolved into giggling and strobe lights and Henry's mouth on mine. This wakening was not unfamiliar: this one was worse than usual.

Peering over the side of the bed I saw the screwed-up remains of my few clothes: three pairs of pants like black snowballs, a bra dangling in an unlikely way from the window-sill and a skirt, two shirts, tights and shoes in a pile under the window. It seemed there had been no time even for Henry to say 'shall I clear out a drawer for you?' I moved into his shabby but airy flat a week after meeting him and had abandoned most of my things at the flat I shared with a friend. 'Must make a trip back,' I mouthed, stretching my arm dozily along the side of the bed.

At first I thought Henry had rolled over and embraced me without my noticing. The arm lying along the edge of the bed was strong and white and covered with dark hairs, not excessively so, but enough to be sure it was a man's arm. I wiggled my fingers. The fingers on the big hand at the end of the arm wiggled.

I giggled. It hurt my throat to do it. I moved the fingers again, noted a ring glinting on the index finger. I recognized it as the one I had found for Henry on an antique stall in Barcelona (another of our torrid city breaks – spent almost entirely in the hotel): dark silver, and polished in such a way that it shone only dimly.

What a dream! I turned in the bed, and found that a woman was lying next to me. She had dark, almost black, hair fanned out over the pillow and a mouth where the top lip protruded over the bottom one slightly. She looked familiar. I was sure that I knew her. Her eyes were closed, she was resting peacefully on her back, her arms out of the covers. Her nails were bitten neatly, exactly as I did mine.

'Henry?' I whispered. I felt the face I was inside lightly with my hands as though I was blind. I felt bristles around my jaw, Henry's strong nose, the straight wall of his forehead.

The girl beside me opened her eyes and turned to me, and frowned.

'I'm having a really strange dream,' I said. It was Henry's voice. The girl stared at me. 'Me too,' she replied. I touched the smooth round white of her shoulder. It felt cool and electric against my fingers.

'Are you in there, Henry?'

'Yes,' the girl said.

'Weird dream.'

'Yes,' she said. 'Although this feels like my dream.'

'Do I look like you?' I asked. 'You are definitely me.'

'If I saw that face in the mirror, I would know it was mine.' Seeing my own smile made by someone else jolted me.

'How long do you think it will go on for, this dream?' I asked.

'I don't know. We could go back to sleep and see if it's all right again when we wake up?'

I agreed. 'Here, I'll hold you while you sleep,' I realised I was the bigger of the two of us and rather enjoyed the novelty. 'And please excuse me if I feel my own breasts while you're asleep.'

Henry laughed. 'I wouldn't blame you if you did. I've always enjoyed them.'

**

When I woke again, the bed was empty. I stumbled out of bed to the full length mirror. There I stood: a tall, disheveled but handsome man in a T-shirt (*I've been to Margate*) and pale blue boxers. I moved my arms and the reflection moved with me.

40

I smiled and Henry's gorgeous face broke into a smile.

The bedroom door opened behind me. Jill walked in, wrapped in a green towelling dressing gown, her face pale.

'I don't think this is a dream,' she said.

★★

We sat opposite each other in the kitchen, a mug of Jim Beam in front of each of us. It was 9am.

'Was it something we drank?' asked Jill, faintly.

'I drank Carlsberg,' I said. 'I don't know about you.'

Jill rested her head in her hands. 'This is insane. I have to go to work on Monday. I can't go as you.'

'Maybe it will have worn off by then.'

We both took a huge gulp of whiskey. I noted the fineness of my fingers and the strength of my hand, and the way it dwarfed the tumbler.

'You look terrible,' observed Jill. 'I always take care of myself. I've usually had a shave by now.'

'Maybe I like a bit of stubble. Remember how I used to like Don Johnson?' Unsmilingly, we shared the joke. 'Perhaps we should call the doctor,' I continued.

Jill ran a finger through her hair, caught an end and twirled it. It was a familiar gesture, my only embellishment being that generally I slipped it in my mouth and nibbled the end before repeating the whole action. She fixed me with a contemptuous stare that was, however, pure Henry.

'But there's nothing wrong with our bodies, is there? I hardly think our case with the outside world is going to be helped by saying we are trapped inside each other's bodies.'

'Good point. In that case I think we should probably try to forget about it for now. Look, it's the weekend. Plenty of time for things to right themselves.' Of the two of us, I had always been the nervy one, but now, strangely, I didn't feel anxious. Jill, however, looked horror struck.

'Forget about it?' she echoed. 'It's not very easy to forget

41

what you've got.' She indicated her body vaguely with a sweeping gesture.

★★

I made every effort to forget about it. I made coffee, placing a cup in front of Jill who sat miserably at the table. I had a shower and I noted the flatness of my body, its new strange contours. I touched my new penis, was shocked by the excited twitch it gave in my hand. This, I decided, would have to be investigated further.

Out of the shower (why had Henry never complained that I had it at a height to suit me and not him?) I wondered if I should attempt a shave. My face felt harsh and prickly. Could it really be any more fiddly than shaving one's legs? I had watched Henry do it often enough.

I covered my cheeks and chin in shaving foam (probably too much). It felt soft and rich; it smelled of Henry. Then I took a new razor and pulling the skin slightly at my ear I pulled the razor down the side of my face. Easy! I opened the bathroom door. 'Henry! I can do it! I can shave!'

Jill looked up at me from the kitchen table. 'If you think I'm returning the favour on your legs, you're wrong,' she said darkly. In euphoria I finished my face, rinsed it with cold water and in a frivolous moment splashed it with aftershave in the manner of the Gillette advertisement.

Back in the bedroom I swerved from the scraps of my clothes to the cupboard which held Henry's neatly folded T-shirts, sweaters and jeans. I picked out a favourite of mine, a faded black one from a U2 concert we had been to and his pale blue 501s. I wore the ribbed Jockey underpants which I had bought him and noted how right I had been to buy them. They were astonishingly comfortable around my newly discovered private parts.

'What do you think?' I presented myself at the kitchen table, arms out. I gave a twirl.

'Don't get too comfortable in there,' snarled Jill. 'That's my body and I'm having it back.' She got up and went into the bedroom. I followed her.

'Don't be like that. Look it's only for a while. Can't you enjoy being me? I think it's happened because we're so close, which means it can change back just as easily.'

Jill was searching the bedroom, a vague, irritated expression on her face. 'I'm not wearing those stupid clothes.' She said. She pulled out a T-shirt from the cupboard and a huge pair of jeans. She undid the bathrobe and let it fall to the floor, exactly as Henry would do, and she stood in front of me completely naked. Her eyes were fixed on me, studying my reaction angrily.

And my reaction? It frightened me. A lurch of desire, and a sense that somehow self control was now negotiable. And beneath it, the recognition we had always shared. In any body I would have reached for Henry. In mine? I went towards her and stroked her shoulder, followed the curve of her breast.

I kissed her. She remained immobile, her hands resting on my arms. My whole body seemed to follow into that kiss. I eased her onto the bed, my head spinning. She did not stop me, nor encourage me. Perhaps the best sex is always an exercise in narcissism, the overwhelming need to find oneself somehow, and in that moment when I held her to me and pushed this new body of mine into hers, I understood. She cried out, but I barely heard her. I whispered deliriously to her, I pulled her hair as gently as I could. I suddenly saw my own need for what it was, something that could finally be satisfied by this person, in this moment. I felt all my incomprehension dissolving, my fear, my need. I gripped her shoulders, to be sure that she was really there.

When I opened my eyes, Jill was crying. They were deep, gasping, horrified sobs. She wriggled underneath me, pushed me off. 'What's wrong –' I began, but then I was interrupted by the telephone ringing by the bed. Automatically I picked it up.

It was Henry's squash partner, Carter. Confused, I began: 'I'll just pass you to him,' but realized my mistake in time. While Jill slammed into the bathroom I had a strange conversation about the last squash game (which I had lost, apparently) and made an arrangement for the next one on Tuesday. If I sounded absent or hesitant, Carter certainly didn't seem to notice. I put the phone down with the kind of reverence one has with a delicate item when one is drunk then I sat back on the white cotton quilt. I tried to curl myself up as I used to do, but my legs were too solid and my huge feet would not tuck in.

I looked up to find Jill in front of me, eyes red, the anger vanished into something else.

'What is happening?' she said, in a small, frightened voice.

★★

Sunday: no change. Early on Jill dragged herself out of bed, checked the awful reality in the mirror and slumped back on the sofa, watching *Breakfast with Frost*. A little later she submitted to the indignity of a bra, realizing she needed it to be comfortable. 'I only know how to take them off,' she mumbled, a tiny attempt at Henry humour. I held her to me, kissed the top of her head where her hair, unwashed and unbrushed for twenty-four hours met in an uneven parting. She complained of aches all over her body but refused the Solpadeine I offered, and sat immobile in front of the television.

It was hard enough to get used to my new perspective, my peculiar new strength, my sense of lightness: I was not sure I could reassure Jill any more that day. I put my head round the door and said, 'I'm just popping out for a bit. Will you be all right?'

'Do I look all right?' she asked.

'I won't be long.' I repeated.

AT THE WATER COOLER

★★

What can I tell you about that day that won't shock you? That I was suddenly invisible, that no one looked at me? I passed the workmen's café: their conversation (I caught a snatch of *fucking Hoddle should be strung up*) continued without a pause, their eyes did not follow me. Not a second's interruption occurred in the demolition of their bacon sandwiches. I had to restrain myself from skipping and from smiling insanely as I wandered into a pub and invisibly ordered a pint and invisibly watched some racing on the huge television. The men around me barely glanced. I caught a bus, and can you understand how amazing it was to sit on a seat that was the right size? My feet on the floor, my back in the right place? The sun came out that afternoon and as I watched the city melt past the windows I was overwhelmed by the sense that it *fitted* me.

When I sailed home late that afternoon the scene with Jill was unchanged except that several empty beercans had appeared on the coffee table. She was watching *The Antiques Roadshow* and was still in her dressing gown.

'Are you ok?' I asked. She did not even bother to look up. I tried again. 'Look, do you want me to wash your hair for you? Shall I help you pick out some clothes for tomorrow?'

She glared at me with an expression of such hatred that I recoiled. It did not look like Henry's familiar contemptuous expression, it was a new one – one of her own.

'Don't be angry,' I said. 'I didn't ask for this either.'

'But you're doing just fine, aren't you? Skipping around in my body as though it was your own.'

'I actually don't see what's so terrible about mine. I'm rather insulted by your reaction.'

'I want to fuck women, not *be* one,' Jill spat. I could see that nothing more constructive was going to be added.

'I'm going out,' I said. 'I'm going to give Carter a ring.'

45

A beer can clattered on the wall next to my head.

★★

It was late when I finally left the bar. The flat was dark and when I switched on the lights I found that Jill had gone. Her clothes and a pile of mine were gone. There was a note left on the table, weighted with a half finished tumbler of whiskey. STAY AWAY FROM ME it said. I scrunched it up and batted it lightly towards the bin. It went straight in. I took a beer from the fridge and sat in the darkness in the living room. It was very quiet. I thought I could still taste her faintly in the air and in the palms of my hands when I pressed my face into them.

★★

I walked into the office kitchen and there she was: hair long now and still unkempt, but with a kind of gypsyish charm. She was making a cup of tea, her back to me. I noticed that she'd bought new clothes, but they were clothes that hid rather than enhanced her body: a loose pale sweater over loose black trousers. She reached for the sugar and I caught sight of her profile, so achingly familiar and yet now made into something completely her own.

I filled up my glass at the water cooler, and when I looked up again she was facing me. We had not met for several weeks, managing through intimate knowledge of each other's habits to avoid one another in the office. Jill had resisted all my attempts to talk to her, not that I had tried very hard. I had spent the evenings with Carter and my other friends instead, and had got extremely good at squash.

But it hadn't gone away, the need for her. She was wearing no make-up and her face was impassive as though she had not smiled in some time. I'd heard through friends and acquaintances (and even from a call from her mother) that she didn't go out with her friends, that she seemed depressed and ill. People seemed to put this down to our breakup, which no one understood and which we had not come up with a good reason for.

I closed the kitchen door, stood against it. 'I still love you,' I said.

'Get away from me,' she said, turning away. I pushed the water cooler against the kitchen door to hold it shut and went to her. I pulled her to me, felt the breath leave me easily at the way she fitted against me.

'Leave me alone,' she mumbled into my chest, not moving.

'If we're together,' I said, 'Then all the pieces are still together. Please, don't keep fighting me.'

I held her away from me so I could look into her face. Her eyes were brimming. 'I hate myself,' she whispered. 'I wish I was dead.'

'No. No.' I hugged her again, ran my hands through the tangles of her hair. 'You are Henry to me,' I whispered. 'Always Henry. My Henry.'

She sobbed against me, quiet, desperate sobs that my body had never uttered when I was in it. I held her until they stopped.

'There's something else,' she said, looking up at me.

'What?'

She took my hand and placed it on her belly, as I used to place Henry's hand to soothe me when I had period pain. She studied my face closely. 'It's ours.'

I took a sip of water, which froze in my mouth. I stepped back, seemingly casually, propping myself up against the counter. 'Ours?' I whispered.

The water in the cooler bubbled, then was still. In the kitchen's electric striplight Jill's face was starkly drawn and determined. It seemed suddenly that I did not know her. Perhaps I used to know her well, but now –

'We will –' I began. 'I will –'

47

Jill ran a hand through her hair, smoothed the sweater over her body. She was leaning against the water cooler, looking not at me, but *into* me. What she saw there she never did say, but after that I couldn't meet her eyes for long. She was like a cat that moved into my life, as if it was its own, outstaring me on the first day, and growing fat and sleek on my envy.

Elephant

When you had the material stacked up, right there beside you, a pile of notes and facts, there was absolutely no reason for being unable to proceed with the next step. William glared silently at the screen. *I'm here, for God's sake!* This inability to write a word had gone on for weeks. His own adage that writing was 99 percent about commitment not inspiration had not helped him shift a single page in all that time.

The house was quiet. It was early afternoon, drawing towards a shining evening. The closed curtains of his study glowed with brilliant sunshine. Writing was impossible for William if there was a view onto the garden, even if it was a plain undistracting one like theirs: a neat lawn which he mowed yesterday, a few flowerbeds in which neither he nor his wife was interested, overcrowded with bruised-looking bluebells.

No one ever described William's writing as creative or important but with things on your mind it was as impossible to write unimportant, forgettable things as it was, he imagined, to write *Ulysses*. William's usual tactic of listing the things that were on his mind as a way of getting rid of them was having no effect, for it was not a list of particular items on his brain, more a sensation of something physically on it, a weight, a *something*, that had – when he thought about it – the colour of haze over a lake on a cool morning.

He glanced at up at the bookshelf above his computer at his girls: *Sophie, Witney, Norah, Becky, Christine, Maria, Britney.*

William wrote biographies of pop singers. Female, alive, young, career-to-date. They were short biographies with lots of photographs, sold in record shops for £1.99, composed from the facts William could glean from the internet. William would have preferred the film stars (male, golden age of cinema) but those had been claimed by someone quicker off the mark, and so William made the best of what he had been given. Recently, some time after *Christine*, he had come to realise it was better this way: if you care too much for your subject your little book might not be able to accommodate all you really wanted to say. To have a lot to say, and then to be unable to say it, in the way you wanted – that would be much worse than this.

The slim volumes reflected the slim lives of his subjects, and his slim interest in them. Apart from the pattern of their rise and decline the girls seemed to him exactly the same: wide-eyed and regular featured, some moderately talented, most not. His current girl was Sandie, the trailer trash orphan who'd become more famous for remaining a virgin than for her singing. He was two thirds through her life-so-far (as she was only twenty this was not a Tolstoyian task) at the point where her first single *Beat Me And Burn Me* had rocketed to the top of the charts. L'Oreal was about to make her their 'face' and there had been one incident of drunkenness and one of a black eye. William was making excellent progress through the life of Sandie. But now he had come to a complete and inexplicable full stop in a way that had never happened before. He could not work out why, except that this haze had descended and he could not seem to lift a thought through its weight.

Laid on his keyboard was a picture he had come across of little blonde Sandie on stage, live at the Hollywood Bowl. It was very recent (he could tell this by her outfit – she was in her gypsy-whore phase), and her face was contorted as she screamed into a tiny microphone strapped around her head. This was so she could be free to dance and gyrate, which she was doing, along side a group of muscled male dancers some of whose limbs could be seen in the picture. Her costume was a variation on the familiar – a tiny pink leather bikini, black thigh boots – and in her case, a diaphanous, skimpy sarong around her flat, muscled hips. The picture depressed him and he was not sure why. Was it her unattainable sexiness? His lost youth? He didn't think so – he had seen so many pictures of girls just like this that they mustered barely a flicker of lustful disapproval, and his own youth seemed entirely disconnected from this writhing overmuscled variety.

William's lips were pressed so tightly closed that they began to ache. He reached up to the bookshelf and took down *Christine*. Her colossal smile, in colour closeup, beckoned him from the cover. Christine was his favourite, the sassy gospel singer who'd made it big; who was delighted by her own booty and sang songs about pride and God. He had laughed out loud writing Christine's life. It was, to him, light and pastel as a bubble, and she knew it too. The eye that glinted out at him was knowing.

Beside him, the telephone rang. It was Ginny, his wife. 'I'm on my way,' she said.

'Right now?'

'Yes, now. I'll be there in twenty minutes.' There was a pause. He heard the sound of the street around her voice. 'Just enough time to think some appropriate thoughts.'

'I'll try,' he said.

It was a twenty minutes that was both long and short. He did not think any thoughts that were appropriate. He remembered instead the twenty minutes he had spent alone waiting for his mother a long time ago. 'I'll be home in twenty minutes,' she said down the phone. 'I have a present for you.' He was six or seven at the time, his mother had been away, perhaps for a long while, he couldn't remember. It was a twenty minutes filled with almost unbearable anticipation. He had remained completely still, the silence buzzing in his head, the *pah! pah!* of the clock on the mantelpiece seeming to stretch the time out even more. And then... a squeal of excitement, her arms around him and something placed on his lap, a wrapped object big enough to fill his entire embrace. Inside the bag – a blue elephant. He remembered now – *a blue elephant*.

He heard the front door open, and realised he had not moved. He got up quickly, composing himself, unbuttoning his shirt. Ginny brought with her the smell of the office, paper and toner, other people's clothes. She waited in the doorway, one shiny shoe pressed against the other.

'I did a test, and it's the right time.'

'Hokey dokey.'

William left the blank page that was Sandie's current life and followed his wife out of the room and upstairs. They each sat down on the bed, took off their own clothes (Ginny leaning over to help William pull off his shirt). William drew the curtains, then they lay down and William made love to his wife. His inability to write disturbed him, made him feel blundering and awkward, but he was practised now in the way this had to be between them, and he succeeded in that he finished within the time he had, despite all the distractions on his mind.

Afterwards Ginny wriggled gently away and lay with her legs propped up on a pillow. 'Well done, darling.' she said. Then, 'I know this isn't much fun for you.'

'I'm not complaining,' he grinned. He noticed his wife's pretty hands and that her nails were bitten right round the edges. She raised a fingertip to her lips and absently nibbled it.

'Did they see you leave the office?' he asked.

'I said I had to get some contracts out of the archive. That can easily take an hour.'

William glanced at his watch. 'You should be back just in time,' he said. 'Not bad'.

'Yes,' she said, closing her eyes.

They lay side by side, not speaking for a few minutes. William felt his eyes drifting shut, his irritation and worry melting away. When he woke, his wife was dressed and standing by the window looking out onto the garden.

'Do you think we should do something with it?' she asked. 'It looks so flat and unloved.'

'Like what?'

'Maybe lay a deck over the whole thing.'

'Let's see what happens.'

'We could sell up, move to Australia like we always talked about. Buy a place without a garden that's right next to the sea.'

'The sea for a garden? Not a bad idea.'

'We could go swimming every morning.'

'And evening.'

'We'd be fit as fleas.' She managed a smile and continued in a cheerful whisper, 'We'd get a lovely tan. We'd be together.'

'Let's see what happens,' he said again.

When she was gone, he tidied the bed and went back down to his study. He pulled the curtains even tighter together and sat down once more in front of Sandie. He put the photograph on one side and rested his fingers on the keyboard. Then he began to type.

When Sandie was twenty and performing at the Hollywood Bowl she fell off the stage, landing on the outstretched fist of Nicole, a plump 12-year-old fan who at that moment had been dreaming of being Sandie. Her eyes were closed and she did not see the moment when her idol came tumbling open-mouthed towards her, and her fist entered Sandie's mouth and broke her neck. The pop world reeled for no time at all, and the hunt began for a biographer, but none could be found, because no one was interested in the life of a girl of very little talent whose life had not actually been lived yet. In fact the only one to come forward was Nicole who had a vast collection of Sandie memorabilia and the beginnings of a 'Life' written in red-felt tip on the back of her maths exercise book. While the world waited for Nicole to grow up sufficiently to string a sentence together, it simultaneously forgot all about Sandie, and her old biographer finally got to put himself out to grass and to idle away the rest of his pointless life —

This little canter left him breathless. He was elated. He blinked, pausing, his fingers taut over the keyboard like the legs of an athlete at the starting gun. To put an end to something — to write the end, instead of these interminable beginnings, that never went anywhere, that drifted over and over, reinventing themselves and yet always the same. His heart was pounding. Taking down each of his girls in turn he finished their stories in whatever way occurred to him: Witney came out of rehab and married her cousin who worked at Wal-Mart, later dying in childbirth. Witney's tomb was a towering shrine in Las Vegas which had her greatest hits on a loop. Norah became an estate agent; Britney had gone acoustic and now released regular albums of triangle music at her own expense… he ended all the biographies with a flourish, pausing only when he got to *Christine*.

Christine was tricky, because he knew that she knew her life was nothing more than an effervescent adventure. The eyes said it all, meeting his from the cover of his book. *I am my own end*, she seemed to be saying. *There's nothing you can add.*

'I know what you need,' he said aloud, in a voice that sounded slightly threatening. He cleared his throat, visualised lighting two cigarettes and placing them in his mouth both at the same time, inhaled deeply, and began typing on a new screen under the heading CHRISTINE.

When Christine was eight she found a blue elephant in a rubbish tip. It became her constant companion. She still has it, takes it on tour with her everywhere.

William smiled, pleased with himself, and the sudden rush of words. His fingers quickened across the keys.

Christine named the elephant Rhoda after her dead mother's favourite TV show. 'It was the best present I ever had,' she said recently in an interview. 'It was fate that I found her.'

Tears filled his eyes. His fingers flew faster and faster. That his career in pulp biographies was definitely over did not matter a bit, in fact he knew with complete certainty that this small gesture was the least he could do. He wanted to give Christine something she had never had, something important of himself. He wanted to give her something that would keep her safe in a brilliant future, that would last for as long print survived on paper, something she could hold onto long after he had vanished from the face of the earth.

Road Kill

At the moment when Lara's husband was delivering the news of his imminent exit to live with a painter named Caressa, a pigeon fell down the chimney. There was a scuffling sound, as though a creature was going to burst out of the wall. It landed head first on the coals and gave a heartbreaking shriek before scrabbling helplessly, smoking, onto the hearth.

Lara's husband, Patrick, put down his briefcase, pulled off his jumper and wrapped it around the bird to staunch the flames. There was a terrible smell of burning feathers and the bird fell into an ungainly silence. When he was sure it was no longer burning, Patrick gingerly unrolled the jumper on the floor. The pigeon sat up, blinking. It eyed Lara and opened its mouth, its spike of a tongue arched, an air of excitement about it.

'I'll put it out,' said Patrick. While he was gone, Lara remained patiently waiting for him to resume the speech that began, 'I'm leaving now.' Before any long journeys she always made her husband sandwiches but on this occasion she was not sure what to do. It would depend of course where he was leaving to. If it was within London, then sandwiches would not be necessary. She wondered where the sandwich limit lay. Perhaps Cambridge. She would wait to see where he said he was going.

Their daughter, Rosemary, was asleep. Patrick had decided to make his announcement at 11.30pm after a particularly protracted telephone call. Patrick came back into the house, bringing a burst of cold air with him that shook the flames of the fire.

'What shall I tell Rosemary?' she asked him.

'I'll ring her in the morning.'

'And do you want a photograph?' Lara leapt to her feet, almost tripping over her nightdress. 'Here, take this one of Rosemary. And this one.' She handed him a photo of their daughter and another of a small boy on a tricycle. 'Where are you going?'

'Manchester. Here is the number.'

Lara wavered and sat down heavily on the sofa. Manchester was the sort of distance that required sandwiches, but she did not think she could make them.

★★

Milana was a florid Canadian whose poetry had been well-regarded about fifteen years ago. She did not write anymore because the sadness, deaths and disappointments which had characterized her early work had mostly come true, and true disappointment without hope of reprieve did not inspire her.

She had met Lara and Patrick during her years in London when she had been living the life she imagined a poet lived: one of passionate affairs and feuds. Along the way, Edward was born, named after the poet she had always been in love with from afar, Ted Hughes. The father, a moderately talented sculptor, had been far too heavy a drinker to change his ways and Milana had decided to return to Canada and to begin again.

When she got the almost incoherent call from Lara, on the night that Patrick departed, Milana saw an escape.

'Let's go on the road,' she said, after a transatlantic pause. 'Let's take the kids and have an adventure.'

The silence at the other end was broken only by a sniff.

'OK,' said a tiny voice. 'I'll see you as soon as you can get here.'

★★

Rosemary looked at Edward. Edward looked at Rosemary. Rosemary saw: a pretty boy, the sort of boy that she had already kissed and had already shared a cigarette with after school, over cans of warm cider stolen from parents and carried around all day until it was warm and flat. He had mean blue eyes and while she would not have categorized them in this way, she recognized them. The boy was slightly smaller than Rosemary and one year older.

Edward saw: a girl who was not pretty, but oddly riveting. She didn't smile. She seemed emotionless. She just nodded at him. In the pocket of her little corduroy jacket a packet of cigarettes peeped out. Her mother stood behind her with her hands on her shoulders, evidently unaware of the stash. Edward said, 'I hate it here. It rains all the time.' And Rosemary, at this, grinned broadly.

Patrick had left Lara the larger of the two cars, an exhausted black Audi whose gearstick had snapped leaving a rather savage point. They packed the boot with clothes and emergency food of various types, Lara was to drive and Milana to navigate. Their destination was Pembrokeshire, Wales, with its wild coastline and fresh air. They put The Rolling Stones' Greatest Hits on in the car and the two women sang along. The children sat silently in the back.

★★

'I think the problem with everything is that I can't drive,' remarked Caressa, half-curled up on the bed like a small, scrubbed and extremely cute pig. It was her cuteness which drove Patrick to distraction. She had a non-verbal warmth which made him want to pack her into an extremely small, soft container and take her everywhere with him. Mad, he knew. Especially now when she was working up to a speech that he knew he didn't want to hear.

'Why do you say that?' he asked.

'Because if I had travelled more, if I'd been more adventurous, then I would know what I want.'

'I can teach you to drive.'

'That's not really the point, is it?' Caressa said. Above the bed was one of her paintings: the view of a city road from a skyscraper. The detail was amazing, and though painted entirely in grey, such were the subtle differences in tone that it felt like a vibrant city viewed through smog. Patrick often found himself gazing at the picture, then when his eyes dropped and he saw her beneath it, he thought that he might explode with hope and happiness. She had gone up Blackpool Tower over thirty times to make the sketches, and yet it was not Blackpool at all. It was a landscape she had entirely invented. Patrick clambered onto the bed, reaching for her, but already her face was heavy with sleep. She slept with the depth of those who can make something out of their fears, and therefore take them away for a time, and of course with the peace of the young.

He waited until her breathing was relaxed and even, then he laid a dressing gown over her curled up form and lay back beside her. He was wide awake, as if it were impossible that he might ever sleep again. At the edge of his vision were the strange elongated colours of a nightmare, one he slipped into every time he managed to sleep. He turned and looked at the painting, lost himself in the tiny figures until he felt calm, until he could remember what it was about himself that ever made him think he could walk out of one life and into another, and somehow carry it off.

★★

As they reached the Brecon Beacons, Lara realized that it was over a year since she had been out of London. No holiday, no clean air, nothing for a whole year. She opened the window and let in a howl of icy air.

'Mum!' shrieked Rosemary. 'It's freezing!'

'But it's so clean!' Lara replied. 'Take a big lungful.'

'What it is, is fucking depressing,' drawled Edward, staring out at the mountains, grey and hunched against the sky.

Milana sighed. 'Don't swear, Edward.'

'You're right,' Rosemary whispered, leaning over to him, so close that corner of the cigarette packet poked his arm. 'It *is* fucking depressing.' She gave him an admiring smile, which he did not return.

'Your country's a shit hole.' He murmured into her ear. She was so close that he could see the shape of his face in the dark centre of her eye.

She bounced back to her side of the car. 'What's Canada like?' she asked.

'At this time of year?' answered Milana, turning round excitedly. 'Oh it has snow ten feet high, and the air is crisp and the sky is clear. It is beautiful, really beautiful. Isn't it, Edward?'

Edward grunted and shifted so that he was looking out of the window. Glancing in the mirror, Lara saw the still-chubby boyishness of his face. She wanted suddenly to stop the car, to run round and drag the boy out, to shake him until he understood something. Understood what? *How much you are loved*, she wanted to tell him, so close to his face that her lips would brush his cheek and her voice would shut out everything that was frightening, and he would be in no doubt. *You are so loved, you stupid, stupid boy.*

The mountains gave way to woods. It was almost dark, and it was beginning to rain. Lara switched on the headlights. The white markings on the road gleamed, and the occasional road sign flashed meaningfully as they pushed on. In the front passenger seat Milana was fumbling with the map.

'When are we stopping? I'm hungry,' Edward whined.

'Not long, darling,' said Milana turning the map round and squinting at it in the fading light. 'It's the next turning,' she added to Lara. 'And it should be appearing around now.'

On each side were steep banks and huge empty trees almost touching over the top of them. A sign flashed by, and Milana screamed.

A piece of the bank had broken free and was rolling into the road. The lights and the rain turned it into a spinning mix of white and black as big as a tree trunk.

'It's a badger!' Lara cried.

There was a terrible thud, and the car stopped dead. Edward was thrown against Rosemary. His head drove into her stomach. Milana turned desperately in her seatbelt to see if her son was all right. The headlights went out and there was a sudden silence, broken only by the rain.

'Wicked!' said Edward wonderingly, peeling himself from Rosemary and staring outside to see the badger.

'Is it dead?' Rosemary asked.

Steam was hissing from the edges of the bonnet. Lara fiddled with the controls in an attempt to switch the lights on.

'I'm going to have a look,' said Edward eagerly.

Lara scrabbled in the glovebox. 'Here – take this.'

The torch sliced through the darkness, the rain swarming in its beam. Edward seemed taller and older than his years suddenly, his eagerness for the macabre gracing him with a look of heroism.

Back home the raccoons tipped over the trashcans and rummaged noisily like beggars. They were so arrogant that they did not run away when you came out to shoo them off. They perched on the trash and stared with their round eyes, like horrible birds. Edward and a friend had taken to shooting them with airguns. The pellets made them scream and jump in the air, and run off dancing. Edward knew about animals when they were hurt, how they found a strange energy, enough to run faster than they ever had. He had never seen any of the raccoons die, though some of them were so full of pellets that blood drooled from them like rain. They always went off somewhere. They never let you watch them die.

Like a spotlight on a field, the torch beam at first picked

out only small circles. The badger's fur was in several layers, the shorter grey fur interspersed with coarse black hairs. Edward moved the torch up and down to try to get a sense of the creature's shape and orientation.

The window wound down behind him. 'Are you okay, Edward?' his mother called. 'Is it alive?'

'Dunno yet.'

The black lump shifted at his feet. It mewed like a kitten, then was silent. Edward suddenly felt the rain coursing down his neck and shivered. He moved the beam of light along the creature's body.

'Mum!'

The badger's eye was wide open and furiously bright in the torch light. Now Edward saw that what seemed like darkness was actually blood, gallons of it, pouring out of the animal from somewhere underneath and onto the wet road. The badger hunched itself trying to drag itself away, but now Edward could see that the back half of it was skewed. He turned away, suddenly dizzy. The creature was snapped in half, its hide the only thing keeping it together. It mewed again.

A car door opened. It was Lara, thin and white in the rain, seeming to absorb whatever light there was. She made her way round the other side of the car gingerly, her hair sticking to her face.

'It's still alive, isn't it?' she whispered. Edward's torchlight trembled across the badger, who now succeeded in hauling itself a few inches.

'Oh dear God, the poor thing,' said Lara. 'We'll have to move it.' She bent over the badger, looking for a place to lift it from. Edward found suddenly that he could not speak, that he was transfixed by the blood that was turning the road to sticky tar.

'Rosemary!' Lara peered towards the car and waved blindly. Rosemary clambered out. 'We need your help with this,' said Lara. 'I think it's a three person job.'

Rosemary hesitated, a black statue in the rain. 'I'll help if I can smoke a cigarette first,' she said.

'What?'

'A cigarette. I haven't had one for hours.'

'What are you talking about? A cigarette? You don't smoke – you're twelve.'

'Oh yes I do.' Rosemary, with a smug glance at Edward took out the packet from her pocket and lit one. She offered the box to Edward, who shook his head.

'We'll talk about this later,' said Lara. 'Right now we have to get this creature out of the way. Edward – can you take this end? I'll carry the biting end.'

'Can't I shine the torch? Someone has to.'

'All right. Rosemary, please can you carry this end?'

The cigarette already half extinguished by the rain, Rosemary gripped the coarse but soft body of the badger. Lara went carefully round to its head. Edward thought he might be sick as the badger yelped. It was incredible that these women seemed to have no squeamishness, as though this agonized animal was nothing especially alarming. *It's sick*, he thought. *Unfeeling and sick*. He shone the beam of the torch half-heartedly where Lara indicated.

'I think,' said Lara, drenched and quiet, 'that we will have to kill it.'

In the car, Milana was fiddling with the ignition and the controls in an attempt to get the lights working. Fragments of poems, whose original provenance she could not remember spun in her head. Then suddenly, a quick turn of the ignition sparked the fog lights into life, and weak light bathed her friend and the children in front of the car.

They made an eerie procession to the verge, the body of the badger sagging in their arms. Edward led the way with the torch. Black blood covered them, smeared on their faces where it had been transferred as they tried to keep the rain from their eyes. The blood shone on their clothes. Most striking of all was Lara. She held the body of the badger tenderly, her fingers moving gently through its fur. All the life seemed to have drained from her face: when at one moment she glanced up, she seemed not to know where she was.

Lara's mobile lay on the dashboard. Milana took it and rang Patrick.

★★

When driving, nightmares are frogmarched out of your head. Thoughts are simplified, shoehorned into the rhythm of mirror, signal, manoeuvre. This is why Patrick loved to drive. He believed, still, that he was an exceptionally alert driver. He was especially careful with his mirrors. If you asked him at any moment what was behind him he would be able to say with impeccable certainty, remembering even certain details, number plates for example, or precise make of car.

The motorway was busy in the darkness, full of lorries on their way down south. Shadowy arms leant against cabin windows; podgy night-faces glared down at him. Patrick had both hands on the steering wheel and noted without really thinking the sign that said London: 200 miles.

After Birmingham, the road quietened. By then it was almost dawn and lorry drivers had pulled into lay-bys to sleep or into Road Chefs for breakfast. The cat's eyes galloped, glowing under the wheels, signs came and went. Patrick was tired, he moved into the inside lane and slowed down. He knew the dangers of being too tired, how suddenly, just once, one didn't look. He knew exactly how that felt, how the car seemed to flinch as it rolled over something, how the shock of not knowing that turned, knifishly, into *knowing*.

The object that hits you at speed at speed can kill you: at the very least it writes off the car. No matter how small it does not let you continue without knowing that it was there, leaving the damage for you to find and remember. But what of the stationary object? What of the small immobile object that you just didn't see? That waited for you?

Patrick's right hand slid off the wheel. Sweat was pouring off him, though he was shivering with the cold. He wiped the hand on his soaked shirt and shook and blinked. He wondered if he should stop, but he knew that Lara and Rosemary were on their way home and if he kept going he might be there before them. He did not know what he would do when he got there, perhaps just hang up his shirts again, make himself a cup of strong black coffee, and wait. He knew what he would not do. He would not look at photographs. When Lara came in he would *not* say, *I only survived because you forgave me.* That was a nonsense. He said the words aloud. *I only survived because you forgave me,* and they stuck in the air, turned the inside of the car to ice. He shivered so much he thought he would lose control of the steering. With one hand he turned up the heating and hot air rushed into the cabin.

Already Caressa seemed a long way away. He thought of her face, the feel of her, the peculiarly possible future they had planned. And it *was* possible, for someone other than him, someone who did not know what he knew, who did not have a secret that only one other person could relieve him of. And when he thought of Lara he was glad of the rhythm of the driving, the way it prevented him from thinking of her properly. The problem with Caressa? He could think of her. Their passion was a real, demarcated thing; he knew where it began and ended, he knew what it meant. But Lara, and beside her, Rosemary... none of it ended where it should.

A movement to the side of the car caught his eye. A huge bird, like an owl was coasting beside the window, low down, wings wide and still. Patrick stared: it was impossible. There was no bird that could fly so fast. He saw the individual feathers of its wings, the round, intent ball of its head. Then it pulled ahead, and vanished.

Patrick was so tired he feared that his eyes would not stay open. Then he saw the bird again, this time standing in the road, facing him, the size of a small child. Its round face housed two enormous eyes that watched him bear down. It was too close for him to avoid and the car slapped into it. He heard the sound, and cried out. He felt the car bump over the bird's body. Patrick gripped the steering wheel, partly to keep control, partly to stop himself from screaming. He knew he must look in the mirror to see what had happened, but was too afraid. The last time he had looked back like that he saw Joshua, his own child, crushed on a toy bike. His wife had crumpled beside the child. Her eyes had looked up at him in the mirror in disbelief.

But then he saw the bird, its wings outstretched, soaring out from under the car, completely unhurt. It was huge and solid and alive and it swept up and into the dawn sky effortlessly. Patrick sped up wildly. The final miles to London flew by. He screeched the car to a halt, fumbled helplessly with his keys, ran into the house and switched on all the lights. When Lara arrived, with his daughter, both of them covered in blood and too shocked and exhausted to speak, he was waiting in the living room. He got to his feet, unsteadily. He wondered why Lara's hands were clasped so tightly together and why his daughter did not smile. He had worked out an explanation for everything, and pressed feverishly on. But his mouth would not open, and he watched in horror as the truth he had come to understand – that there is nothing that a man and his wife cannot overcome – never reached his wife.

ZOE LAMBERT

A Quiet Longing

Consume my heart away; sick with desire
And fastened to a dying animal.
            Sailing to Byzantium   W.B. Yeats

'Feels like rigavivis, never mind rigamortis,' you say. I squash the phone against my ear as rowdy school kids in purple jumpers pile on the bus.

'I'm less stiff after the bath,' you tell me. 'But your Dad dropped some clean washing in the bath water. Those trousers I haven't seen for years.'

You continue with the story till I blurt out, 'Mum, I'm sorry. I can't take you shopping today. Finally got that interview. I'll come on Friday. We'll go out for lunch and *I'll* sort the washing.'

'Oh,' you say. 'Fine.'

Then the bus drives under a bridge and you're cut off, the phone left silent in my hand.

I push away trampled newspapers with my foot, then pull at the window. But it's fixed shut. It's sweltering in here; the chair's itching the back of my legs and my hair's hot and heavy on my neck. I'm thinking about Dad bathing you. I'm not sure how you *feel* when he lifts a tie-dye nightie from your arms – once pink, till he washed it with jeans; how you feel when you steady yourself, one hand on the wall, the other on the sink, as you carefully navigate the floor. Each leg stiff, like stilts. You probably notice the dust in the corner, the grimy towel, the sticky hairs in the sink. You always do.

I'm not sure whether, when you are being helped into the tub by your husband, you are self-conscious of your unsteady knees, the way you can't stand upright. When you lean with one hand on the bath, your breasts hanging, the old scars creasing your belly, I'm not sure if you feel him watching you.

I imagine you Mum – because I'm not there, I'm on this creaking bus, hiding behind a free paper – I imagine you flopping onto the chair-lift and Dad easing your legs over the side of the bath. He puts a towel and soap within reach. 'That's hot!' you exclaim. The tap turned on, the cold water makes a hollow in the bubbles and he rushes to tend burning toast or stagnant washing before school.

The bathroom already steamy, you press 'down' and with a whirr, the chair lowers into the water. When it was installed, you tested it fully clothed. We all did. We lifted and lowered ourselves, up and down. 'A luxury,' you said, laughing. I thought you looked like Botticelli's Venus, especially with your blonde hair. The chair-lift a plastic replica shell.

But having a bath is not the same; you can't relax in the chair, all upright. At least the heat eases the stiffness, submerges and washes away the tight pain. You soap your legs with a flannel and your favourite rose-scented soap, perhaps noticing they need shaving, the hairs long and black and soft. Your legs. Sometimes you pinch them. Hard. Perhaps they are not you. Not yours.

The water round your feet is growing cold, the tap too far to reach.

'Martin. Can you turn the tap off!' you call. You can hear him moving around upstairs. A thud and muffled swearing. You wonder what he's broken this time.

But he is still here. Other husbands would have left. But not Dad. You told me you were his first girlfriend, his only. He was a Beatles fan in those days. You listened to *And I Love Her* when his old Triumph broke down after a date. You danced to it at your wedding. Later, you bought him The Beatles' *Love Songs* album as an anniversary present, though you suspected he preferred the more upbeat tunes. Now, Dad sleeps in the spare room because you're up in the night to use the commode beside the bed. He doesn't want to, but you make him sleep there.

The numbness, you said, can be worse than the pain.

You have invested in jewellery: amber earrings, rose quartz rings, red gold chains. These heavy, glittering stones make you feel feminine again. You wear them like weapons.

You're scrubbing your arms with a loofah. Perhaps to keep the circulation going. Perhaps to keep your skin soft and smooth. You wonder if Dad is making you wait. But no, he's not like that. He tries so hard, but he's just not practical. Though sometimes you suspect he washes whites with blues because really, he doesn't want to wash any clothes.

Marooned and chilled, you call, 'Martin, the tap!' You try to reach it and slip off the seat into the deeper water. It will be a job to get out.

Then he's there beside you with a pile of washing in his arms. Perhaps you notice his hair needs brushing. What's left on top is fluffy and sticks up.

'What did you say?'

'The tap, please.'

He leans over, turns the tap off, and a pair of trousers falls into the water. He tries to grab them, but black socks fall in too.

'Just put them down.' Perhaps your voice is loud, harder than you want. You reach for the trousers that are sinking around your feet. They are black and don't have an elasticated waist; too uncomfortable now. You haven't seen them for years. You wore them to that office party. Must be three years ago. Have they been in the washing basket since then? You remember the restaurant's cheap vinegary wine, the blurry tiredness, then going into the ladies, shaking the puzzling pins and needles in your hands. The muscles in your legs taut and sore. Dad knocked and asked if you were OK and you said, 'I don't know', as you stared at your hands and then yourself in the mirror.

That was just before the diagnosis. Before you took sick leave. Already, the manager was complaining about your slowness, the length of your lunch breaks. 'We need you to keep up,' he'd say. Later, he encouraged your early retirement.

I imagine this like a memory. I was not there. I was on a chugging coach in the Baltics and returned to find you being pumped with steroids in hospital. Your face was bloated and Dad was unable to sit down; he didn't know whether to hold your hand or have it out with the specialist.

The bus is nearing my stop on Candle Road. Passengers work their way to the front. I could get a bus back to your house. I'd be there in half an hour.

I can see Dad pulling the trousers and clothes out of the water, slopping them back onto the other washing. He's not sure what to do with them, these strange objects – that in the process of washing are taking over the house, slipping into his thoughts.

'Sorry, Susanna,' he says. 'I'm sorry.'

His apology irritates you. It's as if he's apologising for everything.

'Put the clothes down,' you say. 'They're dripping down your trousers.'

Dad stands there, staring at the clothes in his arms. He doesn't react. He never reacts. This always drives you mad. You can hear yourself. But you cannot stop. Why had he agreed to become head of Year 7, when he had enough to do? Why doesn't he take more care of what he's doing? How can he organise 190 kids but not the washing? Most of your clothes are ruined.

'Calm down, Susanna,' he says.

He leans over and heaves you back onto the seat. You want to say, 'leave me alone, I'll get out myself,' but you don't. You are already rising out of the water, bubbles sticking to your ankles. He hauls your legs over the edge. They're limp now, weak and unstable after the bath.

He hands you a dry towel and uses one to dab your feet. He gives you a T-shirt and puts your feet into knickers then trousers. He helps you to stand, steadies you and pulls them up. Holding onto the sink and the wall, then the dresser and chair, you make your way into the sitting room, your ankles going over.

You are crying by the time you reach the chair. You don't want him to see it, or perhaps you do. Anyway, you hide your face in your hair. Perhaps he has noticed as he hurries past. Your chest shudders and you gulp for breath. Your eyes and forehead are hot and stinging. You cover your eyes with a tissue and lean on your knees.

I make my way to the front and jump off the bus. Candle Road is heaving with cars and roadworks, and doused in thick fumes. I'm still thinking about you, about how, when Dad has gone to work, you can hear the noise in the room's silence; the ticking clock, the passing cars, a dog barking in the street. A cup of Earl Grey cools beside you and in the hall, beyond the living room door, you see he has left his lunch box behind.

I can hear the words of *And I Love Her* clear in my mind. But I can't quite hum the tune.

> *I give her all my love,*
> *That's all I do…*

'Give us a smile, love,' a workman says in an oversized yellow jacket. I ignore him, and turn to look at the road with its queue of shunting cars. I'm not sure what sustains you. Or how you say to yourself, today I will go on. But you do.

In front of me, the pavement is being dug up. There's a large crater and the workmen stand around it with cups, peering inside as if something was about to emerge. I stop at the barrier and orange cones, confused for a moment. I'm not sure how to get past or which way I should go.

The Breakfast She Had

In the dry season Nadia would dream of rain, soft cooling rain, like freshly welled water that pours away sand from your roots, dust from your eyes.

She does not miss the sand. She would like to turn all the sand in Sudan to glasses. Like the ones she sees in shops. Tall, with glistening stems.

Amina squirms off Nadia's knee and balances between her legs, rocking with the bus. She likes to drink the rain. *Cup of rain*, she will say, with her mouth wide to the sky. *Cup of rain*. Amina is pretty in her uniform, her hair in neat, tiny braids that start at her hairline and reach to a top ponytail. She is watching a woman's handbag by her arm. She loves handbags. The woman clicks it open. Inside are treasures. Bursting purse. Lipsticks. Perfume. Cadbury's chocolate. Nadia wishes she had a handbag of treasures. Her bag is packed with complicated forms, leaflets and a purse of carefully counted money.

The woman is wafting herself with a newspaper. Across the aisle, Nadia notices a boy is shielding his nose. Blood stains his hands and cheek. She wants to offer him a tissue but turns to the window, which is dusty as if Manchester has had a sandstorm. She watches the passing shops, the café, the deli. Her scalp is hot and itchy under her khimar. She pulls the edge of the cloth away from her ear as the bus jerks to a halt. They are flung forward and she grabs the seat in front, holding onto Amina with one hand. The woman's handbag hits the floor, spilling purse and lipsticks. There are mutters and shuffles from the passengers as they right themselves.

Bad driver! Amina says. *Bad driver!*

Ssshhh.

The bus lurches past the parked cars and stops. The driver steps out of his cabin, dazed, as if he has been in there a long time. He says something and jumps off the bus. Nadia wipes the window as he runs into a school car park. She holds up Amina to watch. They will be late for the register.

Her stomach clenches. She could not manage the Frosties this morning. What she wanted was the bowl of warm asida she used to have out by the neem trees with Amina asleep in her arms. Early, when the mists had cleared after a shower in the rainy season, the sun cooking the damp yellow earth and the sky over the heights of Jebel Marra, where she could see the coming sandstorms and downpours. After her husband Masood was up and dressed in a too-hot shirt, already damp under his arms as he walked to Nyala.

Masood was a picture: tall straight back, fat briefcase, tie too tight. But he was too proud to loosen it, proud to work in Nyala. She was also proud of his job in Mana Manufacturing. But he never said what kept him there late at night or what he discussed with his brothers while they ate and she waited in the kitchen. She barely dared to breathe in the thin veil of peace around their house. A veil that did not cover the distant shots or the craters; that did not hide the endless trail of people along the road: women in white mourning, weary men with old rifles.

Masood would walk down the rocky road to Nyala, till he was a spot of white on the horizon. She would already miss him as she watched from the trees and fingered her Taweez. The Ayats-ul-Kursi had protected her mother and grandmother. Masood said she was superstitious. She would still pray the Ayats to him as he walked down the road.

Amina does not remember Sudan or their home or warm asida. She likes Frosties for breakfast. This morning she

sucked them till they were soft and showed them to Nadia on
the end of her tongue. She sighed and rolled her eyes when
Nadia asked her to speak in Arabic, as if she expected her
mother to know her new English words. But Nadia *is*
learning. She wants to read bus tickets, road signs, newspapers.
She needs to read the solicitor's letters and tribunal
determination.

The bus driver is still in the car park. The woman next
to Nadia closes her handbag, glances round, saying, *This is
ridiculous!* She edges through the standing passengers and steps
off the bus. Others follow, pushing to the front.

Amina is hot and fidgeting on Nadia's knee. Her school
is not far. *Come on Amina*, she says. *Let's walk.*

They are late for school, but Miss Miller has not yet taken the
register. They slip into the classroom, trying to be quiet. Amina
heads for the sandpit, but Nadia holds her back and hangs her
bag on a peg.

Good morning, Amina, Miss Miller says. *Good morning Mrs
Abdalla.*

Nadia smiles. *Good morning.*

Nadia usually slips away after the register when Amina is
busy working. Miss Miller has favourite pupils but Amina is
not one of them. At the beginning of the year Amina was
silent, sullen. She did not 'participate in activities.' She bit Miss
Miller's ankle. Now, Amina is in love with her voice. She
screams and shouts and sings to Kylie.

Miss Miller seems agitated. *Sit down everybody. Sit down*,
she says. *They have gone*, she tells Nadia.

Sorry?

Fouad and Tijan. They have been detained. She turns to the
class. *Quiet now. Register time.*

Nadia perches on a tiny chair next to Amina's. The
school had a petition for the twins, Fouad and Tijan, which
was sent to the Home Office. Nadia had carefully and slowly
signed her name.

As Miss Miller says their names, each child stands and says, *Good morning everybody*. She pauses where Fouad and Tijan's names should have been. Amina is eying the sandpit; Nadia has to nudge her to answer. The register finishes and Amina runs over, plunging her hands into the pit, perhaps to feel the cold, moist sand around her fingers. She flings the sand in the air with a shriek.

Amina! Don't throw the sand! Come on, it's reading time.

Outside there is not enough air.

Nadia breathes, but still there is not enough air. She sits on the bench. The playground is empty; waiting for playtime and the children's steps. The wind is busy with crisp packets while shouts and laughter come from an open window. She can hear Miss Miller's voice:

Everybody on the carpet! Come on! Everybody sit on the carpet! Just leave those bricks, Muhammad. Leave them… what did I just say? On the carpet.

On the ground is a hair band. Red and pink and dirty. Dark hairs knotted round it. 'Hair band.' Amina taught her this word. She picks it up and twists it round her fingers. Other words. 'Sandpit.' 'Playtime.' 'Cheese Crisps.' She breathes slowly, in and out. 'Detained.' Amina will wonder where Fouad and Tijan have gone. Nadia does not know what she will tell her.

Last week, there was no air at the solicitor's. The office was dank, the fan chugging, sweat welling beneath her arms and inside her thighs. A fly clambered the window. Mr Williams wiped his pink, shiny forehead.

Tell Mr Williams he is a good man, she said to Amit. *A good man*.

Amit spoke in English to Mr Williams, who shook his head and talked for a while. Amit told Nadia that the appeal had been dismissed on both asylum and human rights grounds.

Why? she asked.

They don't believe you're a credible witness, Amit said. *There is no evidence of your husband's membership of the SLM. The adjudicator doesn't believe you would be persecuted by the militia if you returned to Sudan. Even if he was a member, you're just an innocent bystander.*

I'm telling the truth. They came and burnt my house. The Janjaweed took my husband from his work. She looked from the translator to the solicitor.

What do we do now?

Amit spoke and Mr Williams shrugged, folding her papers.

In the bus shelter's glass Nadia sees a woman in a red-orange khimar, the colour of clay, of midday heat. Beneath it her hair is thinning. She has massaged her scalp with oils, but still her hair has fallen out, leaving patches of skin. She tucks it over her ears and turns from the glass. She is almost glad Masood cannot see her long-shaped head, her dry skin.

Goodbye hair, Amina said when Nadia cut it off. *Goodbye hair.* Then she touched it in the sink and said, *Ooohhhh!* Hands deep in the hair, eyes full of her favourite game, she flung it in the air and around the bathroom, hair landing in little clumps.

Perhaps she will walk home. The street of houses is quiet, deserted almost, shaded by large trees. A breeze catches the heavy branches as she walks past the line of grey bins, spilling cans and cartons. She peers in one at the vegetable peelings and plastic wrappers.

She hurries through a number of streets and down Bromley Road, where there are no trees or greenery. The houses are smaller, red and identical. Her bed-sit is on the second floor of a block of flats. Inside, the hall is dark and cool and the floor is scattered with past tenants' unopened letters. She steps over the letters and treads quietly up the stairs, thinking of how, about this time, her neighbours, Nagwa and Suhair, would visit for coffee and sometimes chat till lunchtime.

Closing the door, she pulls off the khimar and rubs her head. She opens the window and folds the blanket under the mattress. She tidies, picking up tissues and cups, Amina's socks and colouring book off the carpet. She hates this thick, dirty carpet, with its ugly orange swirls. She would prefer a floor she could sweep and wash.

She folds Amina's spare cardigan and carefully places it on their pile of clothes on the table. Next to the clothes, the book of fairytales lies open. Amina likes to tell her these stories. In them, people who disappear come back as swans, frogs, magical creatures, like the tales of ancestors from southern Sudan. She imagines Masood returning to her as a large white bird, soaring down from the sky.

Masood: stood awkward and stiff in his white shirt while their parents agreed to the marriage; his father spoke of Masood's job in Nyala and her father nodded and smiled. Nadia sat quietly, letting the khimar hide her face.

She carries the cups to the sink and washes the dishes, her fingers hurried, clumsy. She drops a bowl. A crack forms. She traces the crack with her finger and sees her hands are shaking. The bowl will fall apart when Amina pours her milk into it, holding the carton carefully with two hands.

The court documents and letters are in a ripped and tatty folder. Sitting on the mattress, she folds and unfolds the papers, the letters, the determination. The words – she traces her finger over the print, the strange round letters, the curving signature. She turns the brochure that opens the wrong way and lets the papers fall onto her lap. Amit's words, Mr Williams' words:

Unreliable witness… appeal dismissed… no proven breach of the 1951 Convention… removal…

Nadia finds the Taweez from under her blouse. The tiny silver book needs polishing; the grooves of the pattern have tarnished. She reaches behind her neck, unclasps the chain and gently takes out the paper. It is yellow and faded, the scroll barely visible.

She sinks back onto the mattress and thinks of how they were under the neem trees when the men came. The empty breakfast bowl on the ground and Amina in her arms. She saw them on the road in their cars, bouncing over potholes. They parked and entered the house, shouting to each other. She took Amina beyond the trees and lay in a crater, a deep hole blasted in the earth. She stayed there till sweat burnt on the back of her neck, till Amina cried and she heard the wheels skidding on the road.

It was the smell of smoke that made her climb out of the crater. Her house burnt easily, thick red flames eating the straw in the roof. They crouched under the trees till one of the neighbours ventured out and brought them water. It was hours till Masood's brother came and took them to Nyala.

Nadia rolls onto her front, feeling the cocooning warmth of her breath on the pillow and the Taweez digging into her palm. She can hear Indian music playing, then a phone ringing on the landing, someone speaking and the pattern of feet running down the stairs. There is a smell of spices; something good cooking. She would like gorraasa be dama, she would like to cook some for Amina when she comes home. It was Masood's favourite dish. He would roll up the flat gorraasa and catch the dripping sauce with his mouth.

She must get up and eat something. She cannot lie here all day. Her legs feel stiff and heavy as she stands. She peers into the fridge and wipes sticky stains from under the eggs she will cook for Amina's dinner. The milk carton is empty, but she will have the Frosties anyway. Nadia pours cereal into the cracked bowl and nibbles the Frosties one by one, tasting the crisp sweetness.

The Skirt

Wheelchairs are ageing. Or so my mother says. They add ten years, like sprouting grey roots. And anti-wrinkle creams won't help. Neither will painting your wheelchair red, but I got my brother to do it anyway. Rob drew Manga style hamsters on the sides. If you're stared at, it should be for the hamsters.

Rob didn't want to come. He hadn't got over the wheelchair thing and he had his graffiti artist image to worry about. Neither did my mother, who couldn't cope with the city centre's crowds and car fumes. She insisted Aunt Joan and Jude from next door took me. They were glad to take turns pushing and have a day out, as long as I didn't mind popping into Ethel Austin's.

'At least you're going in the social services' van,' my mother said, as the care worker rolled me in the hoist from the bathroom to my dining-bedroom. The hoist was a crane that dangled me in material, like swaddling. My mother didn't trust Sue the carer and liked to oversee things and get in the way. She didn't trust the hoist either and waved her hands beneath it in case I fell.

A black skirt and blue V-necked cardigan had been laid out on the bed. It was easier to dress me in a skirt than trousers. I closed my eyes till I could reach the chair with my hands. My arms were stronger. Four months ago, I couldn't lift myself at all. But Sue was still insisting on the hoist in the mornings.

Mum was rubbing my hair dry when Rob knocked and peered round the door. 'Mum, I can't find any socks…'

'Rob! I'm getting dressed!'

'Robert. Give your sister some privacy.' Mum's tone was exactly the tone she used when we were teenagers. Rob didn't mind, as long as he didn't have to pay rent so he could stay job-free and graffiti walls and shoes. 'You'll just have to wash some,' Mum said. She didn't believe in washing machines, but couldn't be bothered handwashing either.

Breakfast was pills with gluten-free muesli. My mother had lined up her pills in rainbow colours. She knew what she'd taken if she went by the rainbow. Mine were large and gritty in my mouth. I struggled to get them down.

'I can't take all these, every day, forever. It's a pill sentence.'

'Bethany. We're all on pills nowadays. You'll just have to get used to it.' She claimed that as a mother, it was her duty to say the truths others only thought.

I couldn't finish my gluten-free muesli. I was on a lactose-free, gluten-free, meat-free, sugar-free diet because no one, not the specialist at the hospital, nor the herbalist, the homeopath or the reflexologist knew what was wrong with me. Saying that, my mother was an advert for alternative medicine. She'd had so many illnesses and the herbalist kept filling and fixing her with tisanes and tinctures. She was hardly surprised when one day I couldn't get up. 'We've all got something,' she said. The specialist stared at me as if I was making it up. The herbalist said I needed to love myself more. The homeopath said I needed exorcising. I screamed every time the reflexologist touched my toes, so he said my feet needed amputating.

It was simple. A metamorphosis. Or so I said.

I woke one morning and could not get up. I could not move. I shifted my arms in the sheets, heavy as if in a half-dream. An ache hummed down my back. Then hot, sharp pains pushed through the post-drunken fog. I tried to move one leg at a time. Wrenching back the covers, I saw my legs hadn't budged. Panicking, tugging at the sheets, I called and cried to my housemates. The room was freezing. The boiler had broken again and I could see that the patch of mould in the corner was spreading, grey-green and furry. The top of the poster from the comedy festival I'd performed at was unstuck; it curled over, baring its white side. I pushed away the stool leg and empty wine bottle. I phoned Gemma, a housemate who rarely went out in daylight. She stumbled into my room, still in last night's clothes, orange lipstick smeared across a cheek. She panicked so much she couldn't dial her phone. I had to call the ambulance myself.

The gluten-free muesli was awful. It was puffed rubber in rice milk. I pushed my bowl away. 'You're not leaving all that,' my mother said, mixing her tinctures. I shifted in my wheelchair. The pain was a warm ache today.

The bell rasped. It had always rasped. We never got round to fixing it, and neither had any of my mother's boyfriends. She went for men that didn't fix things unless they were political. The last one spent his Saturdays dressed as a grandma, disrupting Burger King outlets. Granny Action, he called it.

'That will be Joan.'

Joan was all packed for our day out. She showed us a satchel with crisps, a flask and sandwiches.

'We're going to Market Street,' I said. 'Not Blackpool.'

'I know. But it will be a long day. And they charge the earth in those coffee shops.' She lowered her voice and said in a confiding way, 'Have you got your pads, you know?'

'Of course,' I said and pushed myself back from the table. 'You don't have to go on about it.'

'Moody this morning, isn't she?' Joan said to my mother, who was dropping agnus castus into a glass of water.

I spun round, clanged the table leg and pushed out of the kitchen.

The dining room had been converted into my dining-bedroom when I came out of hospital. I hung onto my room in the shared house, but eventually had to let it go, as I couldn't get up the stairs. My bed was where the old, scratched dining table used to be. I'd insisted on bringing my bookshelves, but most of my books ended up in the cellar.

I hadn't bothered to sort out my stuff, as that would mean permanency. I'd torn up the comedy festival poster since I wouldn't be performing again. Some things I couldn't bear to look at or throw away; my ex, Matt, had colonised Radiohead, (perhaps he identified with *Creep*), Kafka's *Metamorphosis and Other Stories*, and my Eddie Izzard videos. They were all memories of him.

My mother's charity shop ornaments still cluttered the mantelpiece. She liked odd, bargain finds, such as carriage clocks that had no hands or told random times. She rescued lone plates and chipped figurines from obscurity. I was sleeping in an Oxfam rejects graveyard. But with the willowy china ladies and brass bunnies were the new objects in my life: the hoist, the pads, the wheelchair, the tray for dinner in bed. They seemed to match Mum's wallpaper. Green and yellow triangles stained with ancient 70's smoke, which had throbbed and blurred into intersecting Tetris patterns during the past few months. I'd see myself floating from the bed and out of the pain and swimming through the triangles.

Aunt Joan had hidden four air fresheners amidst the figurines, as if my room was now particularly prone to odour. I threw the air fresheners in the bin, then took them out and placed them in a neat row on my bedside table, like four soldiers against smells.

My mother didn't clean; she liked a Miss Havisham atmosphere between boyfriends and she claimed dirt was good for the immune system. She didn't trust electrical appliances (except hair straighteners), so the fridge was rarely switched on. As if to make up for it, Aunt Joan was a cleaning fundamentalist. She knew dusting made the world a shinier, glossier place. Yesterday, she'd hoovered my room thoroughly, in short, harsh movements, as if dust was my real problem and she could solve it. My mother called her a 'dust-crazed bourgeois housewife.' Joan called her a 'dirty flea-bitten witch.' Mostly, they argued over what to do with me.

I didn't know what to do with me.

I wriggled my right toes. Movement was coming back on my right side. In the mirror I dabbed on lipstick and brushed my hair. It was straggly with split ends. I did look older. Especially in this skirt. I'd bought it from a vintage shop, thinking it looked retro. It looked catalogue, with the dark school material and voluminous pleats that reached to my calves. I didn't know why I'd let them dress me in this skirt. I hated it. I really hated it.

I found some jeans on my clothes rail. I put the brakes on my chair, undid the button, leaned on one elbow and tried to pull down the skirt. It was no good. It wouldn't go down. I yanked at the zip, hearing a satisfying rip. I rolled to the bedside table and rooted for scissors in the drawer, then cut from the waistband to the hem and wrenched the skirt off.

The skirt sprawled on the floor, black and ripped.

I'd have to lie on the bed to get these jeans on. I'd practised lifting myself. That was the easy bit. The hard part was getting the jeans up over my thighs. I lay on the bed and pulled.

I was gasping, out of breath and doing up the zip when Joan rushed in. 'What are you doing?' she cried.

'I'm fine. I'm fine!'

Her hands hovered over me. I pushed her roughly away. 'I'm fine!'

'Well,' she said. 'Well…'

'I'll be ready in a few minutes.'

I had some money in my purse. Twenty pounds. My mother had my cash card. Twenty would do. I could hear them in the kitchen. Joan was huffing as she put the dishes away. Mum was talking about global warming and Joan was saying she wouldn't mind, but her legs were still pasty white. Then Joan said, 'She's moody this morning. You should have heard her snap.'

'Why?' Mum asked. 'Were you fussing again?'

'No! Perhaps she's heard from *him*.'

I pushed myself out of the dining-bedroom and to the front door. I tried to hold the door open as I went out. It banged against my wheel. I listened. But they were busy arguing.

'It smells of mouldy cheese in here.'

'Don't you dare spray any chemicals!'

At least there was a ramp down the steps. The only way was to let go. I pulled on the brakes and stopped myself how I used to stop while roller-skating – with a hedge. I giggled as I picked off the leaves.

I wondered if I could make people laugh in a wheelchair. Would I have to rely on slapstick?

The warmth was brimming outside. It was too hot for Manchester, even for July. The social services' van drew up, large and cumbersome on this road of oak and beech trees and old rambling houses. I rushed past. Someone called my name. I ignored them with a smug feeling of rudeness as I clattered over the broken, uneven pavement and round the trees that seemed to burst from between the slabs.

There was a bus stop on Delaney Road North. My arms were already tired and the movement was catching my back, the ache reaching into sharper, harder pains. At the kerb I halted. It was really high. I turned and went backwards, feeling the wheel go over the edge. A car beeped. It was right behind me. It beeped again and screeched off.

I was shaking. What if I couldn't get on the bus? What if it didn't have disabled access? I crossed the road, but couldn't climb the other kerb. I'd have to stay on the road till I found a driveway. Another car blew its horn and I tried to steer close to the pavement, circling each car.

'Perhaps it was a freak occurrence,' the specialist had announced when I last saw him, as if I was some kind of weather. 'Not everything,' he ruminated, 'is known to man or science.' I wondered if he'd been talking to my mother. 'There is evidence of neurological damage on the lower spinal cord, perhaps sustained after trauma. Have you had some kind of accident?' he asked. 'The notes mentioned there was extensive bruising on your lower back…'

'No,' I said. Nothing. No one.

He folded his arms and waited for more. I looked away and wiped something invisible off my skirt.

I'd boxed up the fragments: the wooden stool beside me on the bed, its leg broken and bent; Radiohead playing in another room; the flashes of pain through a drunken blur; the murmured sounds of him talking to a housemate on the stairs before he left.

On Delaney Road I joined the queue at the bus stop. They were fretting, glancing at watches and squinting at the timetable. My eye line caught belts and girls' bare midriffs. A little girl in a pushchair watched me, curious perhaps, at seeing an adult in a chair like her. Faces turned to look. I focused on my hands and knees, and scratched at the red paint on my chair.

The bus drew up. The queue crowded at the door and piled on. Someone lifted up the pushchair. I edged closer and waited. When he saw me, the driver sighed. 'Full up, love,' he said. 'Already got the pushchair.'

An old man next to me stepped up. 'What do you mean? There's room,' he said. 'Can you all move down? Can you make some room!'

I could feel myself blushing. The bus driver wiped his forehead. The bus lowered and creaked till it was just higher than the curb. The old man pushed me on. 'There you go love.'

'Thanks.' I didn't look at the driver, just said, 'Return to Piccadilly.'

'It's free.'

'It's okay. I'll pay.'

'No love, the machine's broken. Just get on.'

I turned to find the rows of people staring. It's a kind of stage, I said to myself. I parked in the wheelchair space, catching a woman's bag and ankle. 'Sorry,' I said. 'I'm sorry.'

I closed my eyes. They were burning and prickling. Squeezing the bridge of my nose, I gulped and tried to focus on my breathing. I couldn't cry. Not on a bus. I needed some of my mother's flower remedies. I could picture her knocking back a whole bottle since they're distilled in brandy. 'Herbal fix it,' she'd say. 'Never mind Jim'll fix it.'

What I needed was to get back on stage. Perhaps I could be lifted or flown on, like in pantomimes. With pin-on wings. I thought of sketches I could do about today, about the skirt and the hoist; the rainbow pills and tinctures.

I opened my eyes and looked back at the crowded bus. I watched a man snoring with his mouth open; a woman in a red headscarf, whose little girl was wriggling out of her grasp; an old woman talking loudly; the newspapers trampled under the feet of passengers that swayed and shifted as the bus jerked and started. I thought at least my wheelchair was red. At least I wasn't wearing that skirt.

These Words are No More Than a Story About a Woman on a Bus

The woman heading towards you is old. You're not sure how old. You don't spend long guessing. Old will do. You watch warily as she makes for the seat next to you at the back of the bus. She's wearing a beige anorak. From a distance it looks respectable. Up close the coat is stained, the cuffs are grimy, and inside the collar is streaked and grey. She sits down and you shift slightly, placing your briefcase on your knee. You open it and flick through the letters and bills you picked up from the mailbox. But it's too early to contemplate bills, so you roll yourself a cigarette for the walk to the office and wonder where you left your antihistamines. The woman is watching you and your briefcase, so you close it carefully and glance outside. The bus is caught in traffic on Candle Road. It's shuddering and shunting round the bollards.

They threw letters from the trains, she says, as if you were mid-conversation.

Deportees would push their notes through high, thin windows.

What? You mumble. Sorry?

Letters, she says. She begins to cough. Her coughs are harsh and wracking. She wipes her mouth with a stained handkerchief. She grasps your hand, her fingers digging into your palm. You try to free your hand from the scaly feel of her skin. You notice her hands are scarred, the skin stretched shiny and tight. Old scars. You worry about your personal space. She doesn't understand this; her knees press against your suit trousers, her breath is sharp and bitter on your cheek.

On her courier trips, she says, she'd find the notes, frozen and crisp by the train tracks. Sometimes wet with blurred ink scrawls. She'd leave them on the verges, like paper gravestones, with pebbles on the corners. Her father travelled on one of those trains. But she never found a note.

Where's this? you ask, loosening your tie.

Lithuania.

You think of Eurovision. Or is that Latvia? You draw a blank.

Her name, she says, is Elena Vidugiryté. She frowns at the ceiling as if she is picking a story from the air. Jonas Zemaitas, she says. Jonas Zemaitas.

She will tell you about Jonas.

You're not sure you want to know about Jonas. Or why she is telling you. Perhaps you should get off the bus to escape her, but your hangover plus hayfever won't let you stand. You rub your eyes and grunt.

This is all she needs.

Jonas, she says, was the commander of the Southern Partisan District. She met him when she joined the partisans with her brother, Jurgis. They volunteered after their father, the Mayor of Ukmerge, was deported, after they were moved from their villa to a tiny cottage on the edge of the town.

But it's the end she remembers, she says. The end.

The last time she saw Jonas she was delivering a message to his group in the forests near to Ukmerge. She was a messenger, a courier, between the groups of partisans in the area.

She remembers, she says, that the only noise was the rain on the leaves and the soft crunch of her boots on the forest floor. Around her the trees were tall and spindly, with a canopy of leaves, leaving the grass yellowing and patchy underneath. She remembers climbing over a fallen branch. She clutched her skirt. It was sodden and heavy and water trickled down her neck. She was so wet she wanted to cry.

She should have been used to creeping through the forest at night. But she wasn't. The darkness scared her; one of the strange, jagged shadows beyond the glow of her lamp could be a *velnias* with their riddles and their tricks. Or worse, Russians. They searched the woods for the partisans with their dogs and their lamps and informers' lies. They were picking off the partisans in ambushes. A week before, three in Jonas' division had been captured and taken to the prison in Vilnius.

Elena tucked in her scarf. She wanted to be by the fire with her mother, a glass of vodka and some fried bread. Her mother had begged her not to do this. Jorgis' decision she had not questioned, but Elena's she couldn't understand. It left her alone at night, sleepless and praying with a small illegal cross.

By day Elena and her mother weaved for the collective. The former weavers, women who now had authority, examined and criticised their work. They'd throw their cloths on the floor of the cottage and wipe their boots on the weave of bourgeois wives. They'd grip and squeeze Elena's hands and denounce them as not the hands of workers.

Her mother would retell the old myths as they weaved, especially the tricks *laumes* would play on women like that. *Laumes* loved weaving, but when they were mistaken for bourgeois wives, they'd cast a spell on the spiteful women's thread, so it continually unravelled. Every cloth the women touched fell apart.

You find yourself half-listening, even though passengers are glancing over and raising their eyebrows at the woman's loud accent. You can feel the beginnings of a headache and the itch in your eyes is unbearable. You give in and rub.

Don't rub, she says.

On each trip she had to go a different route. That night she skirted round the mounds of unmarked graves. The soil was still fresh and she'd heard the dead had dug the pits themselves. Then she followed the stream northeast to where

Jonas and his group were camped. The note almost hummed in her pocket, the words heavy and resonant against her hip. She was not supposed to read it. Not supposed to know. But she had. She always did. In case it said something about Jonas or Jurgis. And this one did.

She could hear barking in the distance. Barking meant Russians and their dogs. But it was far away. She stopped and listened. There were voices. What was that? '*Pasmikst, pakabakst?*'

She was shaking, but it was them of course. They weren't far. She followed the voices till she saw the lights of their cigarettes and the low burning lamp.

Elena came out shyly, and stood on the edge of the clearing. '*Labas.*'

'*Labas*. Did you bring any *cepelinai?*' Jonas asked, approaching her.

'Just bread. Sorry. And some ham.'

Last time she had hugged him. This time he didn't wait. He was already under the tent with Feliksas and Pranuté. They were wet and bedraggled in their patched overcoats, with pustules and sores on their faces. They barely said hello. Elena saw that the second tent, where the others had been, was empty. The roof had collapsed on one side and was covered by yellowing leaves. Underneath a puddle had formed and four stones had been placed there, like graves.

'Come over, then. Get under here.'

She walked round the puddle in the middle of the clearing.

'You could fish in that,' she said and crouched next to Jonas. She handed him the message and the bread and ham. They bit into the small loaves, barely chewing large mouthfuls. She watched Jonas read and eat at the same time. Then he focused on the bread. His face was streaked with dirt, yellow decay edged his teeth, and his knuckles were cracked and sore. His hands were shaking. His hands always fluttered and fidgeted, touching his forehead and his neck. The few times they had walked into the bushes together, she'd stroked his neck till he was calm.

Jonas read the note again, and tucked it into his coat pocket. She watched to see his reaction, but he just looked cold and tired. She edged nearer and took his hand.

'Are you alright?'

'Yes.' He freed his hand and scratched a weeping bite on his wrist.

Before, she thought, they would have been married by now. She tried to imagine him indoors, sitting at a table, the stove burning, and in another room, a neatly made bed. She tried to picture him standing by the fire in the old villa. She couldn't. In her mind, he drifted out of the window and floated into the woods, as if he were a *laumiukas*.

She knew that he grew up in a village south of Vilnius and that he'd graduated from the Kavnas Military School just before the war. In an old military photo he'd shown her, he had close-cut blonde hair, a smooth shaved chin and a wide open smile. She'd asked if she could keep the photo, but he said no. It was too risky.

They had met seven times. That was all. She'd sewn special epaulettes for his coat. He loved them. She'd brought him as much food as she could, sometimes taking from her mother's larder or saving him the meat from her plate. On her missions, she wasn't supposed to dawdle, but immediately return with the message. Jonas would walk with her for a little of the way. But after a few minutes he'd become fretful and want to get back to the others.

Elena wondered if he thought of her when she was not there, or if she disappeared from his mind, like a *laume* at the end of a tale.

The last time they met, they'd argued. Usually, she stayed quiet. That night, she couldn't. Jonas had said that the Lithuanian government had just given into the Russians. It had been weak. They'd tried to bargain, but were tricked and either sent to Siberia or shot. That was no loss; they'd done nothing for Lithuania. And everyone knows not to bargain with devils. Elena thought it was more complicated than that. Things always were. She'd said this and he'd sneered. That was the talk of conspirators, he said. Things were never so complicated as not having a choice. Capitulate or fight. They should have fought. There was always a choice. He was angry. She didn't know how someone could stay so angry all the time.

'Not always,' she said. She was thinking of her father, locking himself in the mayor's office till they came for him.

'Women,' he said. 'That's a woman talking.'

'Do you have a reply?' she asked as he fingered the note. Jonas nodded and scribbled, sealing it in an envelope.

'You should get back. You must be tired,' he said.

'Yes. I should.' She crouched, as if to stand. 'Goodbye then,' she said and then more loudly, as if pointing something out. 'Goodbye, Jonas.'

She walked across the clearing. He was leaving. He had to take the regiment further south, to group with other divisions near Vilnius. It was out of her area. Too far for her to walk. Leaving, like that. No goodbye, nothing. As if she were nothing. She was angry then. 'Jonas?' she said, even though the others looked up.

'What?'

'When will I see you?'

'I don't know.'

'You were going to go? Just like that? Without saying anything?'

'Why? Have you read the message?'

'No, I…'

He turned away. 'You should go,' he said.

She grabbed her lamp and ran into the woods. He didn't follow, even though she looked behind to see if he would. She walked, holding the lamp in front of her, its pool of light flickering. It was darker here, the foliage thicker. She wasn't sure where she was. Perhaps she should go back towards the clearing and retrace her steps home in the other direction, past the stream. Then she saw that she was at the stream. How did she get here? It was shallow with stones. She could cross. But the bank was muddy. She slipped on the verge, her lamp shattering and her hands deep in the mud. She lay there. The sound of the water trickling was soothing in the dark. Further along – she wasn't sure in which direction – the stream was wide and nearly still. On a bright day, the sun would shoot through the leaves and branches, the trees casting dark shadows on the water.

She didn't know whether to go back or follow the stream. She pulled herself out of the mud and wiped her hands on her skirt. She wanted to return to the clearing, but there was nothing to be said. Tomorrow, she'd continue weaving with her mother and again the day after that. She'd carry on delivering messages but Jonas would be gone. The message. She slid the note out of the envelope. She tried to read the words but they were blurred. His hands had been shaking and the scrawl said nothing. She folded it in the envelope and carefully put it in her pocket.

She heard barking, far off. She listened and eventually she heard guns. She heard voices, shouts and more shots. She should run, get away, hide. Perhaps they'd look for her as well. But her legs were weak. She huddled against a tree, her knees to her chest, shivering.

How had the Russians found them? The others could have talked. There had been rumours about the prison in Vilnius. Stories of a room where they made you stand naked on a small ledge above a floor of ice. But she didn't believe they would talk. She held onto the tree trunk, her cheek pressed against the smooth, wet bark. From somewhere she could smell smoke.

Later, she got up slowly, and feeling her way, she walked back to the clearing. The clearing was not hard to find. It was lit by a dimming fire where the tent used to be. Footprints and tracks scoured the mud. All the equipment, the bowls, the blankets had been dragged into the fire.

She didn't get home till morning. Her mother had not slept. She was waiting in the kitchen, pacing up and down. She bandaged Elena's hands and gave her a large vodka. You will have to go, she said. You will have to leave.

The bus shudders and stops. You grab the seat in front of you. She grasps your forearm, her fingers crinkling your sleeve. Passengers are staring out of the windows, muttering to each other and rubbing at the glass. The driver seems to have disappeared. You worry vaguely about being late for work. She uprights herself and examines her scarred hands, turning them in front of her.

She can see Jonas, she says, coughing. She can always see him, even now, crouched in the tent, biting into the hard loaf, his hands fidgety, unsure. And later when she dragged him from the fire and laid him on the ground in the clearing. The epaulettes she'd sewn were black and burnt.

You try not to stare at her hands. You shift in your seat. Clear your throat. Glance down the bus. Some of the passengers are queuing to get off. Through the window, you watch them trailing, one after the other, past the school railings, to the bus stop at the end of the road.

You turn to her, clasping your briefcase, ready to leave. You're not sure what to do with this story, or what to say to Elena, the old woman sitting beside you on the bus.

The Stop

Candle Road

Three more roads and he'd be at the school. Everyday he drove past the railings. Each time he would shift into first, slow the bus to a crawl and watch the children being unloaded from special vans. The vans had lifts at the back that lowered them in their wheelchairs. Other children got out from side doors. They would run or hobble to the entrance, led by teachers.

John would watch from his window till a car beeped or a passenger called from the back. Sometimes passengers would mistake his stop for their stop and crowd at the door.

The air on the bus was damp, cloying. John pulled at his collar and the back of his shirt. He'd take off his jacket, but the wet patches were embarrassing. The passengers were pushing to the front, all jabbing the buzzers, as if the bus wouldn't stop till they'd pressed one personally. At the bus stop they piled on and off. The ticket machine had broken a few roads back, so John was just letting them on. They stared at him surprised, as if it was a trick.

Candle Road was jammed. Yellow cones and barriers everywhere. He wondered what they were digging up. He wondered where they'd dug this bus up. From a bus scrap heap? It was a wreck. It kept stalling and conking out and he'd have to turn the ignition a few times.

John always looked for Michael when he passed the

school. He hadn't seen Michael in two years. Not since he'd moved in with Jennifer and things got awkward.

His ex, Marie, had recently sent him Michael's school photo with photocopies of awards. Gold stars for good behaviour. Success in music and maths. John didn't know what sort of maths Michael could do.

In the photo, Michael wasn't looking at the camera. His head hung to the side, despite the neck-rest. His mouth was open, not smiling. His tongue showed. There were tomato red stains down his blue sweater.

The windscreen was streaked with dirt. He sprayed more water onto it. The windscreen wipers squeaked slowly across the glass and stopped. It made no difference. The grime was thick and grey and opaque. He flicked the switch a few times and gave up. The petrol gauge was swinging up and down and the speedometer hovered on 0 mph.

He had to get to Piccadilly before the engine fell out or something. He thought about kicking all the passengers off. But they looked scary. Like they'd kick him off and drive themselves.

Delaney Road North

John was getting later every day. He just couldn't stay on time. He tried. He tried to drive off as late comers ran up the road and held everybody up. But he always ended up waiting, even though it slowed others down. You had to choose between the one and the many. The one won. They thanked you. The many didn't. All they did was moan. And cough. And from all the coughing and sneezing going on they were all demics. It wasn't even winter. You couldn't have a bus with more ill people on it. No wonder they were moaners.

He'd eventually shown the photo to Jennifer. 'Poor thing,' she'd said through her shiny peel-off facemask. It stretched and crinkled with her skin as she spoke. 'It's a shame for him. What kind of life is it?'

He'd regretted showing her then. Turned from her to put the photo in the back of his bedside drawer. He lay on his side and looked at the neatness of the room: the closed cupboard doors, the parallel Hoover tracks on the carpet, the unlit candles. When she hoovered the front room, he wasn't allowed in, so he didn't mess up the Hoover marks.

There was a huge queue at the stop on Delaney Road North. He sighed and opened the doors. There wasn't room for all of them. He hated that. Having to tell them to wait for the next bus. Last in the queue was a woman in a wheelchair and an old man. He glanced at her again, surprised; she was young and quite pretty, with fair, messy hair. He wondered what was wrong with her. The wheelchair was painted a garish, uneven red. There was already a pushchair and maximum standing.

'There's no room, love,' he said. 'Can't get you in. Sorry.'

'What? No room?' She craned her neck. She didn't believe him.

'It's crammed,' he said. 'There'll be another in a minute.'

The old man behind her strained round, saying, 'Course there's room. Can you all move down? Can you move down?' He sounded like a teacher. People shifted and moved, filling the back seats. John sighed and lowered the bus. The bus creaked and grunted. It could almost have arthritis.

The wheelchair girl was bright red now and her face quivered, like she was going to cry. John looked away and flicked the windscreen wipers again. But they were broken.

Bridgeman Road

The bus jolted, as if it had fallen asleep and woken with a snort. In the mirror, he could see the girl had parked herself. The old man had a seat. That old beggar woman was jabbering on at a passenger again. Some kid was screaming. A girl knocked on his glass. 'Excuse me, do you realise how dirty this bus is? It's disgusting.'

'Do I look like a cleaner?'

'I'll report you,' she said. 'You just fucking wait.'

What kind of life is it? That's what Jennifer had asked. He'd said the same thing to Marie. But he'd also meant his life, her life. They'd been in bed as well. She hadn't had time to change the bedclothes in weeks. She sat up and slapped the quilt.

'What kind of life? What do you mean, what kind of life?' She grabbed his arm. 'It's a life,' she said. 'It's your son.'

'I can't do this. It's not a life.'

'What do you mean you can't do this? Do what? You do fuck all.'

He pulled his arm away. 'You know that's not true.'

'You think he should have died,' she said.

'Where did that come from? I never said that.'

'That's what you're thinking.'

'That's not what I'm thinking.'

'You're thinking he should have died.'

She cried then. Turned over and curled up and cried. He patted her back and stopped when she shifted away. Her wavy hair – he'd always loved how unruly and disobedient it was – was all matted at the back. Then Michael made his screeching, choking noise and Marie went through to him.

He'd just wanted an honest discussion. She didn't want that. So he had to move to the couch. Then back to his mother's. Marie told everyone he was bailing out. Couldn't handle it. Left her because their child had cerebral palsy and learning difficulties.

And they'd thought a baby would make it easier between them. Patch things up. But she'd changed. Marie's world had telescoped to Michael. There was nothing but him. There was nothing but getting him better. And he wasn't going to get any better. You couldn't tell her that.

John had lasted three years after the meningitis. Three whole years. He'd been relieved to have a diagnosis, know what was wrong, what was in store. Marie had repeated the words in different voices: newsreader, market seller. 'Cerebral Palsy. Learning difficulties… they don't mean anything,' she said. 'A label. They don't describe Michael. He's not just that. He's a child.'

The morning John moved to his mother's, Marie and Michael were in the kitchen. Michael was strapped into his chair. He didn't like being in his chair. He preferred to be free and rolling on the carpet. Marie was feeding him puréed something. He could only swallow puréed food, even though he was three, or was it four? Michael didn't like it. Yanked his head away. With his clenched fist, he knocked the bowl to the floor. 'Enough for now, hey?' she said. She'd long ago given up asking John to feed him. John couldn't even watch. It turned his stomach. The puréed something was even up Michael's nose and in his hair. His fists smudged it round the tray.

Marie dropped the bowl in the sink. She didn't turn round. She was wearing her grubby blue dressing gown. He hated that dressing gown. Bought her a silky one. She never wore the silky one. She turned on the tap and stood, looking out of the window. Outside, the binmen were emptying the bins. Her head turned to the overflowing bag by the back door. She told him to take the bin out when he left.

Daisy Street Special Needs Primary

John realised he was passing the school. He braked. 'Sorry,' he called as mutters came from behind and someone cried out. He must have thrown them. He put the bus in first and drove slowly past the parked cars. In the car park, the kids were being unloaded from the vans. At the far end, one boy looked like Michael. A boy in a green coat with a woman bending over his chair. Who was she?

'He has your mouth,' Jennifer had said. 'You laugh like that. With your mouth wide open.' As she walked through to the bathroom, she turned and said, 'You should see him. Don't know why you don't.'

John had forgotten that he was good at playing with Michael. When Michael was out of his chair and lying on the carpet, they'd play with a large soft ball. John would roll it to Michael's hand and Michael would hit it. At first he was disinterested, then he'd hit it and John would bat it back. John thought of the game as a kind of football. He even bought Michael a City shirt to play in. Their other game was High Fives. John would rap Michael's knuckles with his knuckles and cry 'High Five!' Michael loved High Fives. He'd screech his head off.

John put the bus in neutral and pulled on the handbrake. The bus kept moving, so he yanked with two hands. He strained out of the window. He could see the children disappearing into the school.

Yes, one was Michael. He was sure of it. His close-cropped brown hair. The way his head hung to the side. John didn't recognise the coat. Not that he would. The woman was wheeling Michael across the car park. She leaned over him, as if they were in conversation.

John opened his cabin door. 'Won't be a moment,' he said to the passengers.

Then he was out and running to the gate. What if Michael didn't recognise him? For a while he'd visited. Marie would watch them as they played. She'd frown, as if he was doing it all wrong, and say, 'He doesn't understand what you mean,' as he tried to get Michael to kick the ball, or 'He can't breathe if you do that.'

John turned and glanced at his bus. The passengers were watching from the windows. He held up his hand as if to say 'five minutes.' He wondered if he'd lose his job. Or they'd actually drive themselves. Perhaps he should just tell them to get another bus. He didn't know. He half-ran, half-walked through the gates and across the car park. He saw that Michael was nearly at the door.

'Michael!' he called.

Then he saw the boy was not Michael. It was another boy. Hardly like him at all, apart from his hair. The woman was wearing an apron splattered with paint. Her hair was wavy like Marie's.

'Sorry,' he said. 'Is Michael here? Michael Woods.'

'He's just gone inside. And you are…?'

'His dad.'

'Oh. You'll have to go to reception.'

'Right. Okay.' He stood there. Deflated. He didn't know what to say. He stuffed his hands in his pockets. She gave him an odd look and pushed the boy inside.

He turned and walked slowly to the gates. He had to get back to the bus. The passengers would be going mad. They were still peering through the windows or standing at the door. Some of the passengers were walking up the road. John kicked at the grassy verge by the gate and leant against the post, letting his head fall back. He could feel the sweat running under his collar. He didn't know what he was doing here, stood in a school car park.

He saw the journeys he would make, day after day, up and down these roads: the familiar stops, the gasp of the opening doors and the moaning passengers. But Michael was always there, tugging at his thoughts, batting a ball in a City shirt.

John kicked his heel against the post and turned to the bus.

He'd get this lot to their destinations and then perhaps he'd come back. He'd come back and give Michael a High Five. They would rap knuckles. 'High Five!' he'd cry and Michael would screech and laugh.

JANE ROGERS

Conception

My daughter asked me where she was conceived. We were slicing runner beans. The allotment had gone mad and we couldn't eat them all at once. We were going to freeze them in old ice cream containers, we were housewifely and companionable.

Still, I was surprised she asked. I wondered if she had been trying to imagine a time when her father and I got on, in prehistory, before the rows which were all she ever really saw. But when I stopped to think, of course her question was about herself, as it should be: she was interested in the place her own life had begun, not in the messy intricacies of ours. 'Derbyshire,' I said. 'In a beautiful village in the White Peaks.'

'Why were you in Derbyshire?'

'We went away for the weekend, we stayed in a B and B. Hillcrest cottage.'

'You're sure it happened then?'

'Yes. That's when we decided to have children.'

'Look how stringy this one is! The big ones are really old.'

'Chuck the old ones,' I said. The juicy tang of cut beans filled the kitchen. 'There's plenty more.'

'And you got pregnant the minute you decided?'

'Yes. Astonishingly.'

'How d'you know?'

'I just knew. And the date you were born proved it.'

She laughed. 'So, it was a romantic spot?'

'Not really. It wasn't what I was expecting when I booked it.'

'Why?'

'For a start it wasn't a cottage. It was an Edwardian semi. And it wasn't on the crest of a hill, it was more in the depths of a valley.'

Lizzy laughed. I thought about the weekend, and wondered how much I might tell her, and whether knowing it would make her happy or sad.

The man who answered Hillcrest Cottage doorbell was slight and sandy-coloured, fast moving, eagerly smiling. He was glad we were early because he had to go out; he'd just show us the room then leave us to it. We must help ourselves to tea and drink it in the conservatory at the back, where we could watch dusk fall. In the hall lay a defeated-looking black Labrador. It raised its head to stare mournfully at us then got up and slunk into the kitchen. The hall was tiled, with one wall covered by mirror. The mirror reflected us back to ourselves surrounded by cardboard boxes piled almost to ceiling height. To get to the stairs I had to push a child's scooter out of the way with my foot.

Our room looked out over the garden. There were twin beds although we'd asked for a double, so we rolled our eyes at each other. There was a cheap white wardrobe full of extra pillows and blankets, and a skirted dressing table with assorted soaps. There was a neatly handwritten breakfast menu on flowered notepaper.

'Everything alright then?' he asked hurriedly. 'I'll leave you the key. I'm – I'm visiting someone in hospital so I'm not sure when I'll be back.'

'We'll be going out to the pub to eat,' said Mark. 'Should we –?'

'Yes, please lock it, no one else is staying. And can you lock up when you go to bed? What time would you like breakfast?'

'Eight-thirty? Nine?'

'Shall we say nine? I may not be back tonight. There's

towels in the bathroom.' He was already fleeing down the stairs. A minute later the door banged. We stood listening, heard the dog's nails clicking on the tiled floor as he circled the hall then flopped down again. We were all alone. We laughed.

'He couldn't wait to get away!'

'Where d'you think he's going?'

'I don't care. Want to test the bed?'

'Let's have a bath. If there's really no-one here...' We were giggly like kids left home alone. It was a nice bathroom, big and square with a huge frosted window and a claw-footed iron bath. There was a thick powder-blue carpet. We ran a foamy bath and frolicked in it. A couple of times we stopped and held our breath in case someone had come in – but the house was empty, all ours. Mark wrapped me in a towel and dried me tenderly. We didn't make love and I remember the flutter of excitement in my stomach, because we wanted to but we were both waiting until something had been decided. And neither of us said a word about it.

We put our clothes on and went down in search of tea. The dog barely lifted his head to glance at us; a thoroughly disgruntled dog. The kitchen was big and well appointed, a Rayburn and a gas cooker, plenty of cupboards and work tops, everything you'd need to run a B and B. There was a plastic box of kids' toys in the corner, and a miniature cooking stove, with dolls' size cups and saucepans balanced on it. Mark put the kettle on and I looked in the big fridge for milk. There were two fresh pints, a packet of bacon, six eggs, four tomatoes and a tub of margarine. Nothing else at all.

'Look. D'you think he even lives here? He's just bought this stuff for our breakfast.'

'There are all these toys. Where are the kids?' We looked at each other and laughed at the strangeness of it. When we'd made our tea we went through the breakfast room and into the conservatory, where two budgies in a cage greeted us excitedly and a bored marmalade cat stretched and tested its claws on the sofa. There was a scrabbling sound in the corner; a hamster running on his wheel. 'How many pets have they got?' There were children's colouring books and chewed felt pens piled on the coffee table.

'Big garden. Shall we take a look?' Darkness was already falling, but a sensor light switched on as we stepped out onto a paved area which ran down to a lawn. A table tennis table stood on the patio. Two big rabbits hopped heavily to the front of their cage as we passed them. Over the other side of the lawn were dense shrubs and a dark area that gleamed faintly with reflected light. A pond.

'Probably an alligator in there,' said Mark. 'Eaten the children.'

In the darkness it seemed almost plausible. 'The rabbits think we've come to feed them – look. I bet he hasn't fed any of these pets for the night.'

'If you want to start feeding pets, I'll meet you in the pub.'

'No. No. Of course not.' We turned to go back into the warmth. There were two children's bikes leaning against the wall. I wanted us in agreement again. 'It's like the Marie Celeste. He's seeing someone in hospital – but he seemed so cheery –' Suddenly and very loudly the phone rang. It switched to answerphone after four rings, and we could hear it whirring to itself over its message.

'I don't think he's visiting hospital.'

'Well where are they all? D'you think the wife's taken them on holiday?'

Mark shrugged. There was a TV in the breakfast room. He turned it on to watch the news and I hurried upstairs to get ready to go out. All the bedroom doors were closed but I couldn't resist looking inside a couple. One was a boxroom, very pink and girly, with china and plastic horses on the windowsill, and fluffy toys on the neatly made bed. The next was untidy and anonymous, its single beds strewn with heaps of clothes.

At the pub that evening we looked at maps and planned our next day's walk. We were both drinking quite a lot. I remember thinking the important conversation was waiting to happen: the conversation we had come away to have, the conversation about children. I couldn't raise it. It would have to not be me nagging him or pressurising him, it would have to come from Mark. I imagined him suddenly cracking a grin and going, 'Well, me dear, shall we take the plunge?' I had been wanting to get pregnant for a long time, and for a long time he had reacted with exasperation, as if the idiocy of it should have been obvious to me. But now he had proposed this weekend. He was ready to talk about it.

We didn't, though. Instead we talked about our landlord. We speculated about what he did; administration of some sort, in a college or hospital? But he could equally well be something exotic, racing driver or airline pilot. Or architect, possibly. He was hard to place. We remembered the cardboard boxes in the hall and wondered if he ran his own business, by post. Model trains, I suggested. Sex aids, said Mark. We argued about his age. I thought he was early thirties, maybe a couple of years older than us, but Mark insisted he was forty at least. The man was so boyish and eager and smiling I couldn't see that. There was still something undefined about him. And the house – a big rambling house, it must have been expensive, but it was not expensively furnished. I thought of the incongruous mirror-wall in the hall, the chipboard wardrobe in our room, the battered sofa in the conservatory.

'His wife's probably away visiting her mother with the children. Or staying with her sister while her sister has a baby.'

'OK. And he's arranged to spend the night with his mistress while they're away.'

That made sense but I didn't like it at all. His unseemly haste to get away when we arrived; his doubtfulness about returning before morning. It did make sense. 'But he seems so... decent!'

Mark laughed at me.

We floated further explanations; one of the children gravely ill, the wife staying in hospital with it, the others farmed out to friends during the crisis. But then why hadn't he told us so we could sympathise and help by feeding the animals? Why had he been so cheery and so secretive?

With increasing hilarity we discussed his clothes, his income, what his wife might look like and whether she had a job, how many children there were ('a dozen at least!') and what all their names might be. It was nearly 11 o'clock. I remember thinking this is displacement behaviour, he doesn't want to talk about a baby. I remember making a decision not to raise it now, because it was too late and we'd drunk too much. I was afraid of another argument. Better leave it to the morning.

We walked back along the dimly lit village street and not a single car passed us. Hillcrest Cottage was dark. The light and laughter of the pub slipped away.

'He's not back.'

'No.'

We let ourselves into the empty house. The dog opened an eye but never even lifted his head off the ground. There was a rattling, whirring noise, which we realised must be the hamster on his wheel. We crept upstairs as if we were intruders, and lay like spoons in one of the single beds.

'It's making me feel sad,' I whispered to Mark. 'All these toys and animals – it feels so... disrupted. So abandoned. '

'Don't be sad,' he said. He started to stroke my back.

When I turned to face him I said, 'I don't want to have a house like this. Ever.'

'We won't,' he whispered in my ear. 'We won't, we won't.' When I reached out to get my cap from the bag on the bedside table he put his hand on my arm. 'Leave it,' he said.

'Leave it?'

And that's when our daughter was conceived.

I've thought about it since in different ways. Mostly I think we were just young and shiny and invulnerable. But on bad days I see the whole thing was fraudulent: we didn't plan a future, we didn't even dare discuss our motives. We used Hillcrest Cottage to make ourselves feel better, revelling in our superiority to the cluttered broken household where we found ourselves. We created a child in order to prove we were not like that. And in doing so proved, of course, how exactly like that we were. The flavour of that house returned to haunt me in the dark days of our break-up. The beds strewn with clothes; the disconsolate dog; the dementedly whirring hamster.

Sure enough in the morning we found out the story. When he had served us our meticulously cooked bacon, egg and tomato, none of them touching each other on the plate, and brought in a second rack of fresh white toast, he hovered and asked if everything was OK.

'Fine,' we assured him.

'Good. It's the first time I've ever done a breakfast, you see. It's usually my wife, she does the B and B.' His wife, it transpired, had left him. For a riding school instructor. All he had ever wanted was for her to be happy. The house here in the countryside, the children, the pets, had all been his wife's idea. He worked in the city. She'd wanted to be a real mum, she'd stayed at home to look after them, and earned a bit by the B and B.

'She hardly ever left the house,' he said, smiling at us eagerly. 'She loved it. The kids, their pets, making the rooms nice, cooking breakfast. She loved every minute of it. But then in the summer she said she wanted riding lessons. She thought she could go riding with our daughters.'

'What happened?' asked Mark.

'She told me last week, she's in love with the riding instructor. It came out of the blue. She told me she was leaving then she went.'

'She took the children!' I exclaimed.

'Yes. She's the one who looks after them. I have to go to work.'

We stared at him in silence.

'She was happy,' he insisted. 'We had it all planned out. We did everything she wanted. She wanted them to have all these pets and now –'

'What are you going to do?' I asked.

He shook his head, he seemed puzzled more than anything. 'They're going to move to Essex. He's bought a riding stables down there. I don't know about the animals.'

There wasn't much we could say. We packed up and paid him and wished him luck. I felt close to tears. Partly, I was sorry for him. He seemed not really to have taken it in, the way something that was humming along so happily could fall apart in a day. Also I was emotional about what Mark and I had done. I felt tremulous but satisfied, as if I had known all along it would work out as I hoped. But Mark said, 'I'm not convinced.'

'That his wife has left him?'

'Oh yes, I believe that. But that he's only known for a week.'

'That's why he didn't cancel us. It was too short notice, he didn't know what to do.'

'Think about the dog. A dog doesn't get like that in a week.'

I thought about the dog. After I'd thought about the dog, I thought about the fridge, and imagined him going through it chucking out all the half-eaten pots of yoghurt and the bendy carrot sticks and sweet sticky childish drinks, binning the opened jars and packets, wiping out the food history of his family. And I thought, you wouldn't do that if you hoped they'd come back. I had the edge of a nervous feeling about what Mark and I had done, as if I was getting my way by sleight of hand, as if I was trying to take what could never belong to me.

I thought how happy his wife was supposed to have been. I tried to imagine the house ringing with childish laughter, the pets frisky, a song on the radio in the kitchen.

Instead I saw her stripping the beds after the paying guests had left, and the washing machine churning, and limp sheets on the line every afternoon. Her in rubber gloves, cleaning out the hamster and the rabbits. I thought no wonder she's riding off into the blue. I felt sad for them, but still more than anything I was glad. Glad, glad, glad about my baby.

Which was really, I decided, the only part of all this that was worth telling to my daughter. If I told Lizzy the truth of it, wouldn't she find herself thinking of her own existence as somehow provisional? Might she imagine herself to be the result of a domestic crisis amongst strangers? I wanted her to believe her conception was four-square and planned for. Not the product of whim and atmosphere, but of something more durable. The sort of thing other people construct their lives on: commitment, vision, foundations. Why let her know we were rickety from the start?

'We were happy there,' I said. 'The owners had two toddlers and a beautiful baby, and a whole menagerie of pets. The place was humming with life. It clinched something – we both knew we really wanted you.'

Lizzy flushed and smiled at me. 'That makes me so glad – to know it was a happy start.' Her face was like a flower.

'Me too,' I said. 'Me too.'

Grateful

For what we are about to receive, may the Lord make us truly grateful.

That's at school. When it's your turn you have to scrape your table's leftovers into the bucket. Wrinkled brown gravy dried to the plate but slimy underneath. Cold white potato lumps. Chewed gristle and bits of rind. Everyone leaves prunes and custard thick and yellow dribbling across the dish when you tilt it like two runnels of snot from a kid's nose to its mouth. When you scrape the plates more smells come up from the undersides of the food as it plops into the bucket. You think about the people who are hungry. There's a famine in Ethiopia.

OK. When they talk to you they have no idea. No idea that you might have a grain of intelligence. No idea that you're not just some sad bimbo whose diet went wrong.

I can hear them. They don't even have to speak, they think it so loud. They think I'm stupid. 'Dreadful the pressure on young girls today.' 'Those supermodels have a lot to answer for. Shocking.'

I don't speak to them. Why should I, patronising dicks. I don't give a stuff.

You get peace after a bit. After leaving so many platefuls, so many kilos and tons of food. They're giving up. There is just

121

this clear liquid in its transparent plastic tube. No need even to swallow. This is how the angels feed. Pure.

I can tell you. You're listening. What I see and what I know, alright? First think of bones. They're white. It's the best thing about bodies – that bones are white. Under skin and blood and flesh and all the other muck, bones are white. To know that gives me hope. When the crap is peeled away, when the flesh has rotted back to mulch – the bones are white. *Underneath*, it's clean.

It's like a pointer along the way, encouragement. There will be this clean white skeleton – bleached, pure form. And at last even that will crumble away to nothing. Become dust and vanish.

I didn't ask to be born. I certainly didn't ask my mother.

One of them in the early days trying to be matey and understanding goes, 'Do you blame your mother?'
      'For what?' I say. 'For having me?'
      'For your eating disorder.'
      Do I blame my mother? Sure. For my head my heart my brains my belly my limbs my liver – the lot. Who else can I blame?
      'You're making her very unhappy,' he says. 'She'd do anything to help you.'

I am not grateful. This is my crime I can tell you about. I am not grateful. Sometimes she quotes Shakespeare at me, some old man ranting at his daughters how sharper than a serpent's tooth it is to have an ungrateful child. That's me. Sharper than a serpent's tooth.

I don't want to be. Listen. Really, I am sorry. I am sorry for her pain. But if she hadn't had me, she wouldn't have caused it, the pain. She could have saved herself a lot of trouble.

For what we are about to receive: ten fingers, ten toes, two eyes, two ears, tongue, nostrils, teeth etc. Breathing in and out and in and out and in and out and in and out. Death. May the Lord make us truly grateful.

My mother said you must eat your tea. What did you have for school dinner? Did you eat it all?
The food smells gross. When you leave baked beans on your plate the beans go hard and the dried sauce makes a kind of red crust like blood on my knickers when I used to have my period. It's difficult to wash off.

Some people's mothers make them sit at table till they've cleared what's on their plate. She doesn't make me do that. She says you know there are children who'd be glad of your leftovers. There are children in Africa who have to walk miles for a handful of rice.

The butter is spread on the bread in lumps that have torn holes in it, the bread is fresh and the butter is cold. The greasy lump of butter slides to the back of my throat and my stomach heaves. You've got no idea, she says. God loves all his children, but some are starving and others wasting food. Don't you think that's terrible?

I do. I stuff the bread and butter in my mouth and chew it fast. For what we are about to receive may the Lord make us, truly.

It's the waste. The waste is the thing that's bad. She says it's wicked to waste food when some people go hungry. I can see that. You can see that. Wasting is bad. You waste the food and people in another place are starving. Wasting to death. They want the food but you throw the food away. That's bad. It's like you're spitting on their hunger.

Ha! That's what I think of you suckers who need food! I chuck it away, I despise food!

But the other thing to do is eat the food. Once I've eaten it no one else can have it anyway. What am I saying to the starving people then?

Ha! I'm not even hungry but I eat and eat. You are hungry and you have nothing. Ha!

It's not good either.

When I look at the food and I don't want to eat it I think maybe it keeps better faith with the starving people not to eat it anyway. We're all going to die after all. It's more dignified.

The thing about food is, it decays. I used to think about that when she was telling me about waste. Imagine all the buckets of leftovers from all the houses and schools, poured gloop gloop into tankers and driven and carried at top speed to all the places where people are hungry. When they arrive: disgusting. Disgusting filthy mixed-up stinking muck, not fit to give to pigs, pour it in the sewers. But (I thought). If you eat it, it's the same. May the lord make us truly grateful. In that warm stomach. All those chewed bits. Disgusting filthy mixed-up stinking muck. Where does it go? It turns into crap.

In me or in the bin, where shall I let it turn into crap? There's not really any argument, is there?

I tried to explain to her the last time she came, my mother.

'I don't see the point. I mean I know people are supposed to be glad to be alive –'

'Yes,' she said, 'life's a precious gift.'

'But what am I supposed to *do*?' I shouted.

'If you let yourself be normal, you would be happy. You could go to university, you could get a job. You could have children – that's the most rewarding, fulfilling thing anyone can do.'

I looked at her. She didn't even blink.
At least I've spared someone that. Being my child.

I don't have to argue anymore. I don't speak to them, and they hardly speak to me. I am beginning to fade away, is what I like to think. Perhaps they hardly see me.

But then I get – in the night when there's just a line of yellow light under the door and the little orange light on the drip and I am hidden by the darkness so you could almost pretend I wasn't there. I get this. This *rage*. It fills me up like red juice in a jug.

Why me? Why me who gets the food and not a starving person?

What have I done to deserve it? What did I *do*?

People who want food they should have it, OK? Give it to them. The world is full OK, of hungry mouths to feed. Waiting to receive. Waiting to be grateful. Waiting to do something useful. I am not interested. I am not interested in inserting lumps of dead animal and vegetable matter into myself. I am not interested in being made of living crap. I do not have to be a tube for food, and last for 80 years.

Under the muck of flesh there are bones white as promises. Look. Look at my hand. The finger bones are white and elegant, they are clean, there is no superfluity. Nothing unnecessary. An after-image.

I am not necessary. I do not have to keep making myself up out of lumps of external matter. Who says I have to? It is possible to dematerialise.

I can be nothing.

Can I be nothing? I will be truly grateful.

My Mother and her Sister

My aunt Lucy was married for 49 years, until her husband died. They had five children. Sometimes my mother laughed about her and said we'd have been better off with Lucy for a mother, we'd have had hand-knitted cardigans and a daddy who came home from work. We used to yell 'No! No! No!' and pretend to pummel our mother. She'd laugh and push our flailing hands away, and gasp 'Darned socks! Homemade jam!' Giddy with happiness, Tim and I tried to pull her over or climb up her body. No! No! No! A mother like Aunt Lucy must be pathetic.

When I strain now to see Lucy as I saw her then, it is as a picture in a child's book: a Beatrix Potter bunny-mummy, in a safely rounded patch of colour in the centre of the clean white page; up to her elbow-paws in floury dough, with a cheerful fire blazing in the hearth, and a clutch of little bunnikins merrily playing hide-and-seek behind the comfy arm chairs.

We learned from our mother that nothing is more important than your freedom, and that familiarity breeds contempt. We knew that no one wants to be taken for granted. When her boyfriends came round we made ourselves scarce. I liked it when she had a new one, she'd put the radio on loud and let us bounce on her bed while she danced in her underwear in front of the mirror, and tried on clothes. She worked in a travel agents', and in school holidays we went to stay with Aunt Lucy because she was always at home. We played with our stolid, large-faced cousins and ate Aunt Lucy's sponge layer cakes which she glued together with butter-cream, and we waited for our mum to phone us.

Now Aunt Lucy is 75. She's been staying with me since Mum's funeral; my cousin Alexander brought her, in his car full of hot sticky children, and on Sunday I shall drive her home. Uncle Bill used to drive – Aunt Lucy never learned.

I haven't cried at all, I don't know why. When I tell myself she's dead I can't think anything. I seem to be quite hollow, to have gaps in my head. You think you need to talk to someone but what is there to say. Nothing.

It's rained since Lucy came. My house is terribly quiet. She sits near the TV with the sound turned down, knitting. She knits endlessly for her grandchildren. My mother doesn't have any grandchildren. Didn't have. Outside the rain makes a hiss like we're caught in a radio frequency where nothing is being broadcast, the persistent pressure of the sound makes my head ache. Why did I ask Lucy to stay? Because I don't go back to work till the end of the month and it seemed the right thing to do. She's on her own now in that big shabby house, and I never visited after Uncle Bill died. I owe her. Gratitude or something, for all those summer holidays. Recognition. I thought we might talk; my mother, her sister – there must be something to say. I thought she'd know how to behave, that grief would rub off on me.

But Aunt Lucy is difficult company. She doesn't like the rain and refuses to go out, even to the shops. She seems mildly surprised when I try to talk to her. I always thought of her as an easy, chatty woman, good at small talk and making you feel at home. But she's self-contained and silent, she's composed. Her routine is inflexible; she goes to bed at nine, gets up at half past eight, rests in her room from two till four each afternoon. It occurs to me that she may be ill. She doesn't look like I think she used to look, she's not large or comfortably rounded, but short and angular, the sort of old lady who shrinks right down to the bone. In fact she looks very like my mother, although I swear she never used to. She has a rather sharp, intelligent face, and a habit of making a longish pause before she replies to things, giving considered weight to what she says. She makes me feel like a gabbler. I ask about her children, their careers, marriages, divorces, children; and she speaks of them in a rather distant, disinterested way. When, out of politeness, I watch *Coronation Street* with her, she's more animated bringing me up to date on its plot than she is describing her own children's lives.

And then there's the problem of food. All those meals she cooked for me and Tim, all that good healthy fare: roast lamb with brussels and carrots from the garden, and gravy; shepherds pie; fresh cod coated in crushed cornflakes; apple turnovers with baked custard. She made everything. Pastry, bread, jam, the curtains, the tea cosy and my cousins' clothes. So I forsake the freezer and microwave, and buy fresh chicken breasts and lamb chops. I visit the funny little greengrocer on the corner and buy real potatoes, green beans, a brown paper bag of carrots. I consult recipe books about gravy, but gravy is beyond me. I spend the long afternoon while Aunt Lucy is resting, trying to prepare a simple tea that will look as if I know how to cook. The potatoes remain hard – almost crisp – at the centre, but disintegrate on the outside, into a floury mushy soup. I make strong tea to drink with the meal, that's what she used to have. When I place the food on the table she takes a child's portion and leaves half of it. My house smells like someone else's, the fatty stink of grilled chops, the steam of boiled vegetables. I can't bring myself to want to eat it either.

At night I lie awake and listen to the rain. I think perhaps I don't believe my mother is dead. I am a hot dry island in my bed and I wonder what Lucy is thinking.

⋆⋆

On Thursday the rain stopped and I went for a walk while she rested. Everything sodden, and all along the hedges huge, perfect cobwebs festooned with silver drips. It reminded me of walking to primary school with Tim. Of the walk and what we saw being vivid, insistent; of seeing things without the layers of crackling cellophane or whatever it is that holds me separate and hot and dry in the space behind my eyes.

I didn't think about her tea. At six-thirty I put a frozen biryani and a lasagne in the micro, and opened up some wine. I'd refrained all week because I kept forgetting to buy the sweet white muck I thought she'd like, and it seemed rude to drink what she couldn't enjoy. Wrong again. She drank the rough red with gusto, and shot my last stupid assumption down in flames by choosing the Indian rather than the Italian, and eating the whole serve.

'This is what I usually eat,' I said.

She nodded. 'The food they have these days is marvellous.' The bottle was empty. I opened another.

'You used to cook such lovely food. I think Tim and I survived the rest of the year on what you fed us in the holidays.'

'Your mother wasn't a cook.'

'No.'

She was looking at the table with a little frown on her face; it was the first time we'd mentioned Mum.

'I think sometimes she envied you,' I said. 'Your settled life. Being happily married like that.' I don't know why I said it because I'd never thought it before, never dreamt of it. Lucy glanced at me and I felt embarrassed.

'I don't think so. She was always more hopeful than me. Eternal optimist, Dorothy.'

When I visited her in hospital she had the shrunken childish puzzled face of a monkey. She couldn't believe it; that life was going to kill her. Why is she dead? Why?

'How do you mean?'

Lucy shook her head. 'She was an optimist. She kept looking forward. Thinking she would find real happiness. Love. Something like that. With all her boyfriends.' She took a sip of wine. 'Being married a long time makes you see things differently.'

'You mean you don't think about happiness any more.' My voice sounded harsher than I intended.

She began to trace an invisible pattern on the table-top with her thick yellow old-woman's fingernail. 'William and I – I wouldn't call us happy. But we had an understanding.'

Understanding? Not Aunt Lucy and Uncle Bill. An *understanding*, concerning *working late* and unmentioned blonde hairs on his jacket?

She continued in her deliberate way. 'We understood one another. We had the children and we loved them. When you live with someone all those years: working for the same things, knowing the same people; knowing each other, warts and all – you don't make each other happy. Any more than the worms make the earth happy, or the earth makes the worms happy. That's just the way it is.'

I was relieved about the understanding.

'You *think* about being happy,' she said. 'But your mother never *learnt*.'

'Learnt what?'

'That you can't have it. That the thing you want – when you get it, it's spoiled.'

'But Lucy –' Suddenly I can talk to her, we are leaning over the table and we are here and now. 'Lucy how can you say that? It's horrible, it's Victorian. "Practise self-denial. Don't dare to *want*."'

131

'No,' she says patiently. 'Listen. The wanting — is everything.' She looks up through the kitchen window at the darkening autumn evening. Heavy clouds are backlit by a sinking sun. I see her lips move as if she is testing out what she will say. 'I was in love.'

'With Uncle Bill.'

'Oh no. Well, maybe, once, but too much happened. No, I fell in love later. He had black hair.'

I try to remember Uncle Bill's hair. Nondescript. Maybe bald.

'It was — as if I'd been reborn. As if I'd stumbled out of years of fog, where nothing had come close to me — into a brilliant sharp new world. It was so — vivid.'

I don't know what to say. She drinks her wine and looks at me.

'I met him in the library. I used to go there after shopping, if I was early for meeting the children from school.' Aunt Lucy with her shopping bag full of sponge-cake ingredients and soap. A man in a library with black hair.

'What did you do?'

'He asked me to his house. For tea. At two o'clock.'

'Did you go?'

'I went to the house. Number 32. I went to the gate and I stopped then I unlatched it and went down the path. And he opened the door before I knocked because he'd been waiting, listening for the gate. I knew that. I knew he would be.' She suddenly smiles at me and raises her eyebrows, and I see that her pale old eyes are absolutely swimming with tears.

'I put my hand on the doorframe,' she says. 'Just — you know — to steady myself.' She raises her arthritic claw, to demonstrate. 'And he did the same, his fingers just brushed mine... We were both — shaking —' She closes her eyes.

'You didn't go in.'

'Oh no. Of course not. I didn't go to the library again either.'

'Because of Uncle Bill and the children,' I say stupidly.

'No. No.' She looks at me and sees that I am lost. 'He would have become – ordinary. Just a man. Like your mother's. I've kept that afternoon, all these years. It's the most real thing that ever happened.'

We sit in silence, the kitchen window is black now, and the room feels cold. I get up to draw the blind.

'Your mother was like a child. She never learnt to stop hoping. She thought she could have happiness.'

My nose begins to ache and there is the sudden piercing pressure of tears beneath my eyes. Lucy leans across the table and covers my hand with hers.

'She shouldn't have died,' she says. 'It wasn't right for her to die.'

I cry. For my mother, who wanted happiness. For her sister who knows it is impossible. For myself, for what I couldn't see, and for what I cannot understand.

Salt

A woman lived here who murdered her children with salt. Joyce. She didn't come from here. She came from a city. She spent fifteen years in prison, before she came to the Island.

Her children were one and three, both girls. She didn't set out to murder them. She didn't think she set out to murder them. No. What happened was this.

The little one didn't sleep. She simply wouldn't sleep. In the evening Joyce started by telling her stories, as she had to the older girl. In the end she was just counting.

'Four thousand seven hundred and eighty-four. Four thousand seven hundred and eighty-five.'

When the child's breathing was even and her fluttering eyelids closed, Joyce would stop. Wait. Listen. Then infinitely slowly, put down her right hand on the floor, turn her stiff creaking body to the right, shift her weight onto her knees. She would wait, kneeling on all fours, for the rustling of her clothes and creaking of the floor to subside. Then very slowly, hand against the wall for support, haul her aching self to her feet.

Nine times out of ten, as she inched towards the door, the baby's eyes and mouth would fly open and a yell would freeze Joyce where she stood.

If the baby did fall asleep, she stayed that way for about an hour. Then she would be up again, rattling the bars of her cot, calling, babbling, crying. If Joyce tried to ignore her and remained slumped on the soggy sofa, the crying became wailing became shrieking and the crone next door began knocking on the wall with her stick and the older girl clutched Joyce's legs and shouted 'Naughty! Naughty! Naughty!' and the walls of the room throbbed in and out with every exhaling shriek and indrawn breath and the band of suffocation tightened over Joyce's chest.

When the child slept, Joyce slept; sometimes sitting propped against the wall by the cot; sometimes sprawled on the sofa; sometimes curled on the older girl's narrow bed with the bedclothes twisted into a plait beneath the pair of them.

She gave salt to the older girl to punish her. It was morning and she was at the sink, quietly washing yesterday's dishes, running through in her mind what she might be able to do if the baby slept on. After the dishes she might have a bath; she would gather up the dirty clothes and put them in the machine. She would take the bin down and empty it, if the baby slept, maybe even sweep the floor. Outside there was watery sunshine, a gleam of hope on the wet black tarmac.

Then the older girl fell off a chair. She'd been standing on it, leaning forward over the table to reach a crayon that had rolled – went to set her foot back down on the seat and missed it – fell sprawling sideways, pulling the chair over on top of herself, screaming with fright and shock. Instant stereo from the bedroom.

Joyce picks the fallen girl up by the scruff of the neck, plonks her on the righted chair, bawls into her face.

'Now look what you've bloody done.'

The girl sits snivelling. From the bedroom the screams get louder. Joyce buries her face in her arms folded on the work surface; at last raises her eyes and focuses on: SALT. Before she's thought she's poured a slug through its Saxa red funnel into her daughter's mug; half-filled with water, stirred till the cloud's dispersed.

'Here.' Slamming it on the table. 'Drink that. That'll teach you.'

The girl sips and puts it down carefully.

'DRINK IT!'

'Don't like it.'

'I don't give a fuck what you bloody well like. DRINK IT.'

The little girl picks up the mug and drinks. When she is half done she starts to retch. Her mother picks her up and takes her to the bathroom, stands her in the bath.

'Puke there if you're going to puke.'

The coughing subsides.

'Now get out of my way. *Get.*'

The girl scrabbles out of the bath and runs to her bed. She gets in and pulls the covers up. Joyce stumbles to her room and grabs the screaming baby.

At first it was a punishment. Something she could make them both do, that they didn't like. Force the girl to drink it. Put it in the baby's bottle and let her gulp until she tasted it. Give her something to scream for, that would.

Then she noticed it made them sleep. That first morning, the girl stayed in her bed till noon. If they drank enough to make them vomit it exhausted them and they slept even more. Or it gave them stomach aches and they lay whimpering quietly, squirming in their beds, unable to run around or bellow.

The baby'd drink it without a fuss, mixed in juice. With the older one, she and the girl both knew it was punishment. For making a noise. For spilling something. For being clumsy or untidy or simply in the way. For *being*. And she was big enough to say no, to go without a drink. Joyce slapped her away from the taps and the fridge. When she drank her dirty bathwater Joyce started putting salt in that.

It was never intended to kill them. She didn't know it *could*. Just wanted to teach them a lesson.

Teaching them a lesson is for their own good. Joyce had

been taught lessons. She'd learnt I want doesn't get and nothing in this world comes free. She'd learned not to get above herself and not to ask for the moon. She'd learned money doesn't grow on trees. She'd learned life's a vale of tears. Valuable lessons, needing to be learnt by young children. Joyce was helping them to learn. Helping them not to be like herself; so desperately furiously suffocatingly trapped, so caged and raging, so dissatisfied. They were born bad, like her, and she could teach them to be otherwise. Teach them – herself – a lesson.

When the older one had a fit, her body twitching and convulsing like a fish flipped out of water, Joyce watched with tearful sympathy then carried her, calm and floppy, to her bed; tucked her in and kissed her. Poor little kid. So much pain in life. She might as well get used to it now. Joyce was doing her a favour. Poor little mite; now she was beginning to understand the truth of it, life.

When they were both in bed all the time, it was easy. Poor things. It was for their own good. If they learnt who was boss now it'd stand them in good stead for the rest of their lives. She mopped up the vomit lovingly. Bought fresh orange to put the salt in.

The baby died first. It had been sleeping a really long time. So long that Joyce herself was calm and refreshed, humming as she made herself a cup of tea, smiling at the television presenter, only mildly annoyed by the car alarm that went off under the window, loud enough to wake the dead.

It didn't wake the baby.

The baby was cold to touch. In terror Joyce grabbed her up. Thumped her on the back, tried to breathe into her mouth, ran to the phone, stabbed 999.

It was only when she was being asked her details in the hospital that they found she had another; back went the ambulance – and back again to the hospital, bearing the older child still breathing, but salted down into a coma from which she never would recover.

The salt murderess. At her trial she cried salt tears and said she was only trying to keep them quiet. Why is it on sale if it's a poison? she wanted to know. The prosecution said it was a poison so unpleasant that no one would take it unless forced by measures of extreme cruelty. That the physical sufferings it induced included painful muscle cramps and contractions, a fearful raging thirst, vomiting, diahorrea, hallucinations and convulsions.

'But they drank it!' wailed the mother.

'You gave them no alternative.'

The salt murderess was sent to jail, judged to be of perfectly sound mind and a danger to all children.

In prison all children visited her, convulsing up and down the walls of her cell. For fifteen years she lived in a cell where children writhed around her like worms in a fisherman's bucket. For fifteen years she half-lived, numb with pain, blind with too much vision.

And when they let her out of prison she came to live on the Island. A fellow prisoner had talked about it. About the emptiness, and the gleams of light on water. From the prison library Joyce borrowed books on gardening.

She found an empty cottage; semi-derelict, forgotten, owned by someone on the mainland. She lived there lightly, with planks and polythene sacks across the roof, an untidy plot of onions and potatoes at the back. Walked to the post office each Thursday to collect her giro, buy a few groceries. Never bought salt. Spoke to no one. Sat in the evening and the morning staring out to sea, the sides of her head unpeeled to the horizon, not a wall not a child in sight.

Dreamed by night of glistening saltchildren floating in

white from the sea, sculpted and still as bars of soap in the moonlight; saltchildren, a million crystallised tears. They floated gently as ice in the black water, bumping and nudging in to shore. But in the morning when she looked they were gone, there was only the brown seaweed bobbing to the surface, and the occasional grey-backed gull.

Salt preserves and salt destroys. All life sprang from the salt-soup of the sea but her children are dead as rocks and hang as heavy about her heart. It was a madness, an accident, an impossibility. How can there be a thing done, which can never never be undone? How, in a botched and transitory life, can one thing become irrevocable? She sees she is only that: a saltmurderess. All the rest of her life is void. It was all, waiting to become that, and living to regret it. Clouds and seaspume are the colour of salt; sea air keeps the taste of it in her mouth: even here, there is no escape.

Then one frosty salt-grained night there's scrabbling at her propped-up door; scrabbling and snuffling and shuddering sobs. Head still full of salt-mummies she stumbles to the glassless window and leans out. A young girl is battering weakly on the door, fists upraised, hair salt-silver in the moonlight.

'Here,' Joyce calls. Her voice has scarcely worked for sixteen years.

The girl comes blindly to the window – Joyce helps her over the sill, leads her to her matted pile of bedding, wraps her in a blanket. When the girl has snuffled and burrowed herself to sleep, Joyce lies beside her, curling her body around the warm question-mark of the girl's blanketed back.

It is no mystery where she comes from. She's the younger daughter of old McCaulin. Who that night had tried with her what he'd been doing with her older sister the past five years. Only the nine-year old did not lie sickened and still but fought like a cat, scratched him to bleeding and ran two dark miles to the safety of the nearest dwelling: Joyce's.

And there she stayed. Walking down to get the boat for school, and back in the evening to Joyce's cottage. When McCaulin was out fishing she fetched her things from his house, and two of his six geese that she said were hers. They kept them in the ruined front room and they made fine watchdogs. She showed Joyce how to collect winkles, and where the blackberries were. They ate no salt.

And when Joyce sat staring out to sea in the evening, the girl coloured in her exercise book on the flat rock beside her; or if it was wet, they sat either side of the driftwood fire, and made up spooky stories.

Joyce never spoke of her children; nor the girl, her father. This was their life. And when Joyce lay curled around her island-daughter's sleeping back, she had no more dreams of saltchildren, but dreamt instead she was at the prow of a boat, with the warm sun on her face and chest, sailing forward into the light.

Meanwood Sally

On a warm day I like to sit here on the bench under the trees and stare at the old place. Meanwood Park Hospital. The mental place, you know. The care assistant drops me off while she does my shopping, she's a good girl. This is where I used to live. Been closed about ten years now.

Did my son survive? I hope he did. I wish he did. Don't you know?

That'll be Lucy, poor soul, the American girl. I reckon she's been grievin' since before I were born. They come to me, you see, they all have their stories to tell. Sometimes I think I've spent my whole life listening!

Ernest so much wanted a child. That boy, the boy I see under the beech tree – thin, in a brown jacket, what's his name?

Doctors said I warn't fit to rear a child. I dare say they were right.

Dinna thee lock me up! Dinna thee lock me up!

Hush Jack, hush, wait a minute my love. Sometimes they do distract me, they're like children wantin' attention – when living folks won't listen, they get fretful. But I have to tell you about this place first, Meanwood Hall as was. You'd call it a stately home. Beautiful tall windows that flood the rooms with light, and stone golden like a lion. The drive sweeps in from the right with huge beech trees facing – it's a picture.

I don't think Ernest ever came back here after I died. It was let to strangers, and after that it stood empty – empty as a shell.

They sold it to Leeds Corporation an' it were an asylum then for 70 years, home to the likes of us.

I can't see distinctly. I can't see the time after I died, it's like looking through a wall of water. The distance between things is distorted, straight lines bend and skinny things swell. It's different every time I look, there can be a figure by the tree I'd swear, a boy – and next time he's just vanished. Ernest wanted a son very much, I would like to think he had one.

Listen dear, you must wait. I can't tell it all at once, you'll get me in a muddle.

I've waited so long...

You've waited over a hundred years, my love, a mite more'll make no difference. Let me tell the tale. They sent *me* here about a baby. Well. The doctor said I was mute. 'She has lost the power of speech,' he said. 'Stubborn, more like,' said my mother, 'and a disgrace to her family. There's nowt wrong with her but stubbornness, and when I find out that lad's name her dad'll beat the living daylights out of him.' Well, my dad couldn't have done that, could he? Couldn't have beat the living daylights out of himself. 'Don't you breathe a word,' he says, and he called me a bad name. So I didn't, I kept my mouth tight shut. They tried soap, they tried salt water, they tried the electric shocks. In the end the doctor said, 'Best place for her is the asylum.'

Dinna thee lock me up!

I was scared too, Jacky my love, but in the end it warn't so bad. Look at all the friends I made! All the tales they told me... I lived here nigh on 50 years. I listened but I never spoke, not till they told me my dad was dead. 'Do you want to go to his funeral?' they asked. I found a word then: 'No'. I didn't like it when you couldn't listen... when they all started crying or shouting... but when we're alone they'll talk to me. And sometimes now, I'll reply. Ralph whose legs were blown off in France, he likes me to bring him blackberries. My best girl Jean, she used to cry for me when she had nightmares, and I'd even sing to her – oh, the air is thick with them, can't you hear?

Mi Ma gev me to't loony bin. Ah niver arst for nowt, Ah did as Ah were bid, kep mysen hid in't shed, but she sez, Th'art a big lad now Jacky, Ah canna keep thi. *I said dinna thee lock me up in Meanwood!* But, no *she ses,* tha frightens folk wi' tha fittin'. *They niver see me! Ah cries, but she sez* Ah canna look arter thi all mi life, what'll become of thi when Ah'm dead an gone? Tha's gotta go now an' mek best on't, tis all new theer, a proper modern place. Meanwood Park Colony for Imbeciles and Epileptics, theer's doctors and all sorts to look arter thi. *Ah dinna wanna go theer, Ma, dinna mek me go to no Meanwood!* Stop tha chelpin, tha'll be frothin at mouth soon enow.

He come before me – Jack. He was one o' first –

I can hear him, is it him?

No my love, I don't think so.

Are you sure?

You are Lucy, aren't you?

Yes. Lucy Beckett.

Well they say Jack's mother was Eliza in the laundry.

There must be some mistake.

When did you come to Meanwood, dear?

I came to England in 1884, I was 20 years old. It was so dark! Dark all the time, as if the day never properly started, and before it could start, it was night again. In the evening when the fog cleared I saw three girls under the railway bridge, young girls, younger than me, one with a baby. I said to Ernest, we have to help them, and he said it doesn't do to give them money, they only drink it. Then in the spring we came to Meanwood Hall. The parkland was so fine! Great beech trees, smooth and bare as seals, silvered in the light. Ernest wanted a son. But children don't come to order; what was I supposed to do, take tea with his mother every afternoon? I told Ernest I intended to help those girls. I worked with the vicar; we raised funds for a Home for Waifs and Strays, we appointed staff, we even had a laundry purpose built. We took in 30 girls employed in laundry work and machine-knitting stockings. I was so proud! I'd call there every morning, to hear them do their reading. I swear Ernest was jealous. He thought because I loved them, I would never have a child of my own to love. As if my love could be used up! He said I was too busy, I was over excited. But there were always a dozen things to do at the Home, teaching the girls embroidery, planting the kitchen garden, finding a situation for Mary where they would let her keep the child... because we couldn't, I had the other girls' reputations to think of. I never had a moment to spare!

When t'fit comes tis dark black as coil-'oil. T squeezes mi till Ah canna draw breath, Am an ant unner a clarty great clog – till mi skull's kibbled. I canna see, Ah canna tell thi only when Am shooken and blinded and ivery bone in mi body's loose in's socket then 't lets mi go. An Ahm at peace then like a newborn babby floatin in a pond. Tis the one good thing abart fits, peace n quiet after, like yon peace in't bible, as passeth all understandin'.

Shi took mi down Meanwood. Ah were that scared Ah canna tell thi, ah were heart-sluffened, it took me weeks to come to.

Who was it took him? Who was that woman?

I heard it was Eliza.

But I did have a baby. After 7 barren years. Do you not believe me?

My dear, we all had babies, and some kept 'em and some lost 'em, and some took it very hard. You shouldn't grieve so after all these years, Jack wasn't unhappy, whoever lad he was. Listen,

That Meanwood were a great white room wi winders t'ert sky an ivery man n lad a bed to hissen. Next to mine were Johnny, he ses, tis better'n what you think. *Dahnstairs they gi'ed us porridge. There was clatterin an shoutin an crying, Ah was feart to look. A lady come to our table, she tells us* you lads'll do haytimin' terday, Jack, foller Mister Wade. *What! Can us go out then? Aye lad, says Mr Wade,* tha's stong enow, tha can lift a hay rake, eh? *We walked dahn a lane wi great trees heavin and shakin in't wind n glishy sunshine spillin through, there war a mighty beech wi a trunk like a pillar o leet. I says, Tha willna lock us in then?* Nay he laughs, *Why, is tha dangerous? But can Ah come out heer ivery day?* Aye, if tha's a good worker. Eliza's boy, ent tha? *Sometimes Ah have the fits. Ah canna help it.* We're used to that here. Us'll tek care o' thee. *In't field the grass war fresh mown n sweeter n' owt Ah iver smelled, an they gi'ed mi a wooden gripe and Ah tedded an' tedded till mi shouwders ached, an the skillies war singin fit ter bust.*

When I found that I was pregnant I was excited beyond measure. Ernest would have his son, I would have my own baby in my arms, and my girls could play with him and spoil him. I told Ernest that day at Meanwood Hall. The new leaves on the beech trees hung out pale and damp as fresh laundry, and the sun shone gold on the old stone house with its elegant columns and balustrades, and Ernest talked about getting the place done up. He was just back from London, full of news: I was waiting to tell him my own. We're walking back down the drive when he says, I climbed that beech when I was a boy. *I can't believe he did, the trunk is one vast gleaming column, not a foothold in sight. We pause there in the shade, and that's when I tell him. His eyes shine like the sun, then he picks me up and whirls round and round with me, and I look up at the pale leaves with the light sparkling through, and I think at last we can be happy together! I lived to see my baby boy. I did hold him in my arms. It was three days later that the bleeding began, and the night after that, I died.*

I was lucky having my baby. It was all over in two hours and I never bled at all. I cried when they took him away but they said I wasn't fit to rear a child and I dare say they were right. I might have held him too tight or got upset when he cried, I was only a slip of a girl myself. They give him to someone who could look after him properly. A blessing for both of us really. I was sad at the start but I got over it. There were other girls who took it harder than me, poor things.

It's under that same beech tree I see the boy, sometimes – a tall boy, slender, in a brownish jacket by the silvery beech? I glimpse him then he vanishes –

But can Ah come out heer ivery day?

Mr Wade says he's Eliza's boy. You heard that, Lucy, didn't you dear? Didn't you hear him say that?

But they gave him to Eliza. Did they? Give him to Eliza to look after?

We come back up t'gate an Ah seed what a great hall t'were wi stone columns n round corners, the'd be ower 30 rooms inside Ah reckon. Johnny says, Does tha see yon winders wi bars? That's for t'real loons, as niver see't light er day. *Ah were feart ter go back in theer, out er't sunshine an sweet wind, an wi'out thinking Ah meks a run for't, an shimmies up yon great beech tree.* Ey up! shouts Mister Wade, have we got us a monkey? *Dinna thee lock mi up! Dinna thee lock mi up! He comes and stands under't tree;* No-one'll lock thi up, lad, tha's nowt ter fear. Tha'll be my right hand man. Now come an get thi dinner. *He goes off wi 'tothers, leavin me ter foller, an Ah slides down tree an Ah looks up inter't branches ower mi head, all't leaves war shaking in't wind an light spillin through like skimmerin' water fallin on mi, like bein' baptised.* Tha's nowt ter fear. *Ah lived theer all mi life, tha ken, Ah were Mister Wade's right hand man. Ah knowed ivery tree in Meanwood park, but twas yon great beech Ah loved the best.*

He died before they sent us to Care in the Community, did Jack. He was a happy soul.

Did my son survive? Don't you know?

I don't know about your son, Lucy my love. I don't know about my own. I don't know where they went – where in all the wide wide world.

Did my son survive? Did Ernest have his boy? Is it the boy under the beech...

She'll be back. We all come back, the living and the dead. It's lovely here now. You know what they've done? They've knocked down all the asylum villas and built this beautiful new housing estate. There's young mothers pushing their babies in gleaming buggies on the pavements, it's like – I don't know what. It's like a dream. And the poor old Hall, left standing in the middle, like a lion in a pen, with all its shutters closed and the lawn gone to seed and the rhododendrons gone mad – they're doing it up for luxury flats. Imagine that! Won't it be grand? And the beech trees are standing yet, watching all our comings and goings, keeping all our secrets. I like to see these young folk in their colourful clothes, with their babies smiling up at them. Everyone can be happy these days, can't they?

The Anatomist's Daughters

When my sister rang me she was worrying about a skeleton.

'A human skeleton?'

'Yes.'

'Why have you got a skeleton?'

'I thought I could use it in some way – make casts of the bones –'

My sister Tamsin is an artist. She's made exhibition pieces out of a giant clam and a sheep's pelvis, so a skeleton didn't seem very strange. 'Well what's the problem?'

'I don't know. It's in my kitchen. I don't know where to put it.'

'In the closet,' I quipped. 'Keep the skeleton in the closet.' I tucked the phone under my chin while I uprooted a thistle; I was still gardening, in the last of the light. I asked her where the skeleton came from. She had got it from Chris who did his medical training in Melbourne back in 1980. He was splitting up with his wife; his med school skeleton had been kept in their garage. He told Tammy his wife had screamed at him to 'take that damn ghoulish thing away too!'

'Where did *he* get it?'

'I can't hear, talk into the mobile!'

'Sorry, I was just getting a weed. I asked where did –'

'They all had them then – anatomy students, they had to buy a skeleton to study –'

'It's illegal to trade in body parts.'

'Now. I suppose they have plastic ones these days.'

We talked some more about the skeleton and I suddenly visualised it, hanging there, listening to her talking to me. I found myself entering into her predicament.

'It's not hanging, it's not all strung together,' she said.

'You mean it's just a heap of bones?'

'There's a hand connected up, and a foot, and a few of the vertebrae. The rest's–'

'The knee bone's connected to the – ah – thigh bone,' I sang.

'She's a person, Maggie. She was in an old banana box, all cobwebby and dusty. When I opened it up and saw her skull... I had to polish her and wrap her in pillowcases to make her feel better.'

'Her?'

'Chris told me she's an Indian woman.'

'You could bury her,' I said stupidly.

'And if someone digs her up –'

'Ah. A murder rap. You can't get rid of her.'

'No. But I can't just keep her under my bed.'

'Where are the skeletons all the other medical students used to have?'

Neither of us could imagine. You don't go to the doctor's and see them displayed in the waiting room, alongside the doctor's certificates. Or in junk shops or on eBay. Or maybe you do, I've never looked for a skeleton on eBay.

'Dad must have had one.'

'Yes. I remember seeing it at his lab.'

Our father was a professor of Anatomy, before he died.

'Where did they all come from?'

'India. All the skeletons in Australia are Indian,' she told me.

'But how did they get them?'

'Bought them from med school suppliers. Who bought them from agents in India–'

'But where did *they*– ?'

'Dad said they fished them out of the Ganges.'

We laughed then. It was so exactly what he would have said. The combination of slimy corpses, casual racism, and the trashing of religious sensibilities made this his favourite sort of utterance.

'Well,' said my sister. 'At least you made me laugh.'

I thought about our father as I finished my gardening. He would have scoffed at Tamsin. He had no patience for anything psychic or spiritual: he was a rationalist to his core, a despiser of sacred cows. He liked to think of himself as a rebel and identified with every kind of outsider. But he also despised stupidity, and since religion and superstition were, to his mind, stupid, his attitude to most people was one of contempt.

I pondered his character as I worked, then felt angry with myself, and sat on a crate and rolled a cigarette. He was dead and couldn't defend himself. I hauled into my mind the things I loved about him; his passion for books and ideas, his sense of humour which was a scalpel he wielded against every kind of self-inflation. His expert gentleness when we were little; he could soothe a grazed knee, get a comb through tangled hair, comfort with the laying on of hands. He was the best teacher in the world: able to render complex ideas simple without distorting them; a lover of plain English, a great democrat in his teaching. A mountain of good qualities against the mole-hill of his failings. Why was I so bitter?

For childish reasons. For childish reasons, although I was an adult.

Tamsin rang me again a couple of days later. I was driving home from the shitty call centre, I had to pull over to talk to her. 'D'you want to come round at the weekend?' she asked.

'What's up?'

'I want you to meet Indira.'

'Indira?'

'The skeleton. I'm reassembling her. I'll have her strung together by Friday.'

'I don't mind coming to see *you*, but—'

'You think I'm being stupid.'

'I think you're being irrational.'

'I can feel her watching me. It's as if I've let a genie out of a bottle, her presence is expanding.'

'Get rid of her. Take her in to the Anatomy Department.'

'She wouldn't like it.'

'Can you hear yourself?'

'There's so much sadness. She's been ignored for so long.'

'It's *bones*, Tammy.'

'I'm not being funny, she's in my house. I have to figure out a way of living with her—'

'Get a pet. If you need something to love, have a baby or get a pet, and stop being such a fucking flake.'

There was a little silence, then Tamsin put the phone down on me.

Later that week I lost my mobile. I'd stopped at Kulkami Reserve for a walk on my way home from the call centre. My mobile was in the pocket of my denim jacket. It was warmer than I expected and I ended up carrying the jacket slung over my arm as I climbed up Mindiyarra hill. In the distance I could make out a mob of kangaroos idling in the spring sunshine, on the flank of the hill that leads down to the creek. I decided to go down that way rather than back along the path. To begin with I was scrambling through rocky outcrops; then the slope became more gentle, with coarse tufts of grass underfoot. The kangaroos didn't move off till I was pretty close, and I saw a couple of joeys hop back into their mothers' pouches. That always makes me smile.

I didn't feel for the phone until I got back to the car. Then I realised what an idiot I was. The most obvious place for it to have slipped out was while I was slithering down the rocky area near the top of the hill. It was already half past five and I was meeting Jerry at six thirty – and, duh, couldn't phone to say I'd be late. I set off at a run back through the kangaroo pasture (they'd vanished, not a one of them in sight) and up the side of the hill till I came to the area where rocks take over from grass and scrub. Then I realised the impossibility of it. There was no path through the rocks, that's why I'd had to scramble. I stopped. Red rocks and their black shadows on all sides; between them a multitude of cracks into which a small object, dropped, would immediately vanish.

The lost phone bugged me all that night. It was partly the cost of a new one; mostly, the hassle of having to go into town to buy it, and have a different number so nobody would be able to contact me – and having to locate and enter all *their* numbers again. Losing it disconnected me from everyone I knew. I imagined the phone lying on a stony patch of ground, bleating and going onto answer-phone; people leaving me messages I could never pick up.

That gave me the idea. If I borrowed Jerry's phone and retraced my steps, I could ring my own number. The sound of its ringing would lead me to it. My shift at the call centre didn't begin till ten, I'd have time before I started.

In the morning he was grumpy about lending his phone. 'I feel lost without it.'

'That's how I feel.'

'I might get an important call.'

'One of your other women?'

He laughed and pushed me back onto the bed and we rolled there together for a minute, warm and close. 'Why is sex more enticing when there's not enough time?'

'Because you like to know you can get away. Shoo. You'll be late for work.'

We left his house at the same time, and I drove straight out to the reserve. The early sun was still low in the sky, making the red rocks glow like embers and intensifying the smoky green of the gums. I dialled my number on Jerry's phone then held it away from my ear. Silence. In the distance a magpie warbled. I thought I'd retrace my steps so that I could leave the top of the hill at the same point I had done yesterday. Maybe from the top I would be able to identify my route down.

I dialled and listened repeatedly on the way up. Nothing. At the top, the same. The morning sun was beginning to bite, it would be hot today. I sat on a rock and rolled a cigarette and stared down at the jumbled, stony hillside. It was already nearly nine. I didn't want to go to the call centre anyway. Of all the crap jobs I've had that's the crappest. Jabbering at idiots all day long, you don't know them, they don't know you. I decided to try and find myself some sort of outdoor work, gardening or agricultural, something that wouldn't be so – contaminating.

Our father cut himself off when we grew older. Left our mother, left his university post, took himself up to Darwin. I don't know how he lived up there, we were never invited to visit. My mother assumed he'd gone to another woman but I'm not sure that was true. He sent me and my sister a letter saying he wanted to concentrate on making sense of his own life, now we were grown up. I know the letter by heart but that doesn't mean I understand it. He talked about having no more to give us, and said his job with us was done. He recommended that we be kind to our mother (to whom he was sending a monthly cheque) and he hoped we would be happy.

As if. For a long time we were angry, and that settled into a lingering resentment. We would have conversations about how we wouldn't visit even if he invited us. My aunt talked about male mid-life crisis. But time ran on and we never heard from him, not even on our birthdays. It was a complicated stew of feelings; anger and hurt at his rejection, and an embarrassed kind of shame at his behaviour, which was so aberrant, so unfatherly that we felt the need to conceal it from our friends. In my darkest heart I understood that it must be our fault, that he must be more disappointed in us than any other father ever was in his children. It was easier to pretend that he was dead, than to reveal that he simply did not want to see us. In our rare moments of success we felt truculently satisfied that he was not able to bask in reflected glory: in periods of failure and despair we observed bitterly that this was all due to his unnatural behaviour. I used to fantasise about a reconciliation, and how he would try to make it all up to us.

And then we heard that he had died. He was diagnosed with a brain tumour, and they tried to operate and he died. He died on the operating table with a surgeon probing the unfathomable circuitry of his brain.

His death was hard to bear. He had removed himself even further, rendering himself permanently inaccessible, removing the possibility of us ever understanding or of his ever being able to make amends, even if he had wanted. How can people do that? Just die, absent themselves, cease to be answerable? Leaving all those question marks hanging in the air? At his funeral we were stunned and dumb.

Sitting there on Mindiyarra Hill I felt an urge to talk to my sister. But I didn't want to use Jerry's phone; finding my own was somehow dependent on not making a proper call from his. I thought of Tamsin wrapping the bones in pillowcases, and wondered how many spare pillowcases she had, and why she chose them rather than old T shirts. I thought about the Indian woman and wondered if she had children, and if they had been to her funeral.

I once visited Bombay. I stayed in a cheap hotel opposite the back entrance of a hospital. When I woke in the morning there was wailing under my window, and a small crowd with garlands of orange flowers taking delivery of a corpse. It was a woman in a sari, who they carried at shoulder height in a noisy procession down the street. I remember being shocked at the lack of concealment. I caught myself thinking stupid things – that an open corpse on the street is unhygienic, and that I wouldn't want everybody looking at me when I was dead.

Now I wondered what they had done with her body.

You don't get a skeleton from cremation. To get a skeleton you must clean the flesh from the bones, by worms underground, or weather and vultures in the air. Or by immersion in a vat of chemicals. What family signed up for an acid bath?

People do leave their bodies to science. But if *all* the medical school skeletons were Indian... I found I was having gruesome, Burke and Hare thoughts, of relatives not consulted, of absence of donor cards. Of fishing bodies out of the Ganges. I rubbed out my cigarette butt between finger and thumb and dialled my number. Nothing. I got to my feet. It was easy to identify the spot where I had begun my yesterday's descent, to the left of a large jutting rock, and down to where the ground became stony and loose underfoot. Since it was too steep and slippery to go straight down, I must have chosen a diagonal across this. I slithered to the nearest sizeable rock, perched and dialled again. There was a click. I looked at Jerry's phone. It gave one little exhausted beep and switched itself off.

I was so angry I nearly smashed the thing. Here I was on the exact rocky pathless stretch where I knew damn well I'd lost my phone, and I'd used up Jerry's battery calling in all the places where I knew it *wasn't* lost. When the rage faded I put the dud phone into the zipper pocket of my combats, and considered running back to the car. I'd only be half an hour late for my shift.

A great flock of galahs came wheeling and clattering overhead, and as their racket passed over I heard another sound underneath it. A tinny electronic four note ditty. Close enough to touch. I leaned over the rock and looked down into the shadow on the other side. My phone lay exposed like a piece of evidence on the bare ground. I got it on the seventh ring, just before it went to answer.

'Maggie?'

'Tams! You've found my phone for me!' I told her about my lost phone. She listened, sympathising and laughing in the right places. Her voice was warm and bright in my ear. My sister, connected on the end of the line. I apologised for calling her a flake.

'It was when you said have a baby—'

'I'm sorry, I'm s—'

' — you sounded like Dad.'

'I know.'

There was a little pause then she said, 'Alright.'

'Can I come over tonight, and make acquaintance with Indira?'

'It's not a joke, Maggie.'

'I'm serious.'

'OK.'

'OK. I'll bring a bottle of wine.'

I walked back down to my car, my phone clutched tight in my hand. As I passed the kangaroos I shouted 'Whoopee!' but they just twitched their ears and carried on nibbling the grass.

ALSO AVAILABLE IN THIS SERIES...

Ellipsis #1
comma modern shorts

sean o'brien
tim cooke
jean sprackland

ISBN 0-9548280-2-X
RRP: £7.95

An out-of-season seaside town, a library stocked with memories, a man slowly going mad...

Starting in the hotels and suburbs of a down-at-heel coastal town, Jean Sprackland's stories follow a cast of rootless characters, young men and women clinging to tokens of the past, whose lives are so lacking in ballast they become as unstable as the dunes themselves.

Tim Cooke invites us into a very different space: the derelict rooms and vandalised stairwells of an inner city tower-block. From there, each story draws a claustrophobic spiral round the next, following various characters (or is it the same person?) desperate to flee their demons.

Sean O'Brien's stories also spiral outwards – not from a state of mind but a setting: an ornate, vaulted lending library, an edifice from another age, where unlikely users and chance items found in stock lead to quite different lamentations for the past.

"Sprackland's stories combine narrative energy with affecting compassion for her troubled characters... she has now arrived as a short story writer. Tim Cooke is another extremely exciting author...bold...and skilled."
– Time Out

Bracket
a new generation in fiction
Edited by Ra Page

ISBN 1 85754 769 1
RRP: £7.95

The latest in Comma's acclaimed series of short story anthologies, brings together 20 of the country's most promising, previously unpublished writers. From the cliffs of Flamborough Head to high rise, inner city madness; from lost loves to the last days of civilisation – the settings and scenarios in these stories captivate and unsettle in equal measure, all the time striving for that most unlikely modern thing, intimacy.

"Such collections are rare and high quality ones rarer still but Page has sourced only the finest material and it's pleasing to discover that, for the near future at least, short fiction is in good hands."
Independent on Sunday

"Fills you with hope for the form... there isn't a bad story in *Bracket* and some are very good indeed."
Time Out

"The stories fizz and ricochet like atoms in an accelerator. They grab you by the ears and give you a good shake." *Mslexia*

"Get with the zeitgeist and buy yourself a copy of *Bracket*."
Leeds Guide

Under the Dam

David Constantine

ISBN 0-9548280-1-1
RRP: £7.95

In the middle of a speech a businessman realises his soul has just left his body. In an Athens marketplace, a jealous lover finds himself staggering through a vision of hell. High in the Alps, a young woman's body re-appears in the glacier, perfectly preserved, where she fell 50 years before.

Entering Constantine's stories is like stepping out into a wind of words, a swarm of language. His prose is as fluid as the water that surges and swells through all his landscapes. Yet, against this fluidity, his stories are able to stop time, to freeze-frame each protagonist's life just at the moment when the past breaks the surface, or when the present – like the dam of the title – collapses under its own weight.

'Flawless and unsettling'
– Boyd Tonkin, Christmas Books of the Year, The Independent

'I started reading these stories quietly, and then became obsessed, read them all fast, and started reading them again and again.... The description of the estuary is one of the best descriptions of the surface of the Earth I have ever read'
– AS Byatt, Book of the Year, The Guardian